PRAISE FOR THE PLAYS OF

DADA WOOF PAPA HOT

"Delve[s] with intricacy and heart into the thorny lives of the proliferating number of gay couples with children today . . . Mr. Parnell's play smartly explores the complex emotional and sexual dynamics of relationships, gay and straight, and how they can evolve (or devolve) once the responsibilities of raising children factors into the equation."

—**Charles Isherwood,** *The New York Times*

"Seriously intelligent and deadly accurate."

—**Jesse Green,** *New York* magazine

"Excellent, clear-eyed, and thoughtful . . . What makes the play most remarkable is how directly it speaks to today's weirdly bifurcated, marriage-and-negotiation gay moment."

—**Jesse Oxfeld,** *Entertainment Weekly*

A tender domestic comedy . . . Parnell accurately covers commonalities between gay and straight parenting, even as he also delves into differences."

—**Jennifer Farrar,** Associated Press

"A provocative and enjoyable topical comedy for today."

—**Steven Suskin,** *Huffington Post*

"Gay drama has traditionally steeped in victimhood: bullying, disease, unrequited love, and so forth. Here, though, gay characters get the long-overdue opportunity to simply be people, neither defined by nor defecting of their sexuality . . . [Parnell] does a superb job humanizing the anxieties of these men, caught between being cultural paragons and being all too human. He deserves real credit, too, for trying to create a new language for gay plays . . . You get the sense people will be talking about *Dada Woof Papa Hot* for many years to come."

—**Christopher Kelly,** *The Star-Ledger*

TRUMPERY

"*Trumpery* is a tightly focused study of Darwin, his family and his intellectual circles in the years just before and after the 1859 publication of his earth-shaking, faith-shattering book about natural selection . . . Mr. Parnell manages to conjure unexpected jokes from the unlikeliest of subjects . . . He also puts firm flesh on Darwin and his colleagues, who might have come across as fossils."

—**Charles Isherwood,** *The New York Times*

"The play makes a sly running comparison between scientists' struggle for priority and the animalistic survival struggle embodied in Darwin's theory . . . Parnell makes [the] personal side of the play riveting."

—**Michael Feingold**, *Village Voice*

"A spellbinder . . . A play of ideas that resonates today as significantly as a century and a half ago . . . As clashing truths enlist us in a thrilling, funny and terrifying combat we must, as human beings, inescapably join in."

—*Bloomberg*

"Artfully written . . . taut dramaturgy . . . damned effective theatre."

—*Variety*

QED

"A seductive mix of science, human affections, moral courage, and comic eccentricity . . . not to be missed."

—**John Simon,** *New York* magazine

"The play itself is a kind of proof, dramatically illustrating how a man who happens to be a genius elegantly and movingly works through the human problem of how to face the end of his life."

—**Nancy Franklin,** *The New Yorker*

THE CIDER HOUSE RULES, PARTS ONE AND TWO

"Engrossing . . . Interweav[es] dozens of compelling incidents and characters so deftly you barely see the stitches . . . an odyssey that has only one major shortcoming: It comes to an end."

—**Misha Berson,** *Seattle Times*

FLAUBERT'S LATEST

"Handsomely stimulating and . . . deliriously enjoyable."

—*New York Post*

"Long passages of tangy, bubbly writing . . . produces what is not only Parnell's wittiest but his most mature work so far."

—*Village Voice*

HYDE IN HOLLYWOOD

Hyde in Hollywood is a sophisticated attempt to raise the persecution of gay men from the footnotes of mainstream history . . . There have been few new plays this year with as much to say as *Hyde in Hollywood* or with potentially as intriguing a way to say it."

—**Frank Rich,** *The New York Times*

"Great depth and unusual resonance . . . Its message is valid for any age when those who would entertain us or lead us are willing to sell their souls to the imagemakers." —**Michael Hill,** *Baltimore Sun*

ROMANCE LANGUAGE

"The creation of a bold writer with an abundant vision . . . *Romance Language* is a spiraling series of interlocking dreams—erotic, fantastic, and patriotic." —**Frank Rich,** *The New York Times*

THE RISE AND RISE OF DANIEL ROCKET

"Even as *Daniel Rocket* becomes increasingly fanciful, it remains unpretentious, and it is grounded in truth about the mutual hurtfulness of children and the need for illusion in their young lives."

—**Mel Gussow,** *The New York Times*

"Bears ardent testimony of Parnell's freshness, originality and gleaming talent." —*New York Post*

SORROWS OF STEPHEN

"An engaging romantic comedy with literary undertones."

—**Mel Gussow,** *The New York Times*

PETER PARNELL's plays have been produced by the Public Theater, Lincoln Center Theater Company, Playwrights Horizons, and the Atlantic Theater, among others. He wrote the new books for the Broadway revival of Lerner and Lane's *On a Clear Day You Can See Forever,* and Disney Theatrical's production of *The Hunchback of Notre Dame* (music and lyrics by Alan Menken and Stephen Schwartz). His play *QED* starring Alan Alda was produced by the Mark Taper Forum in Los Angeles and Lincoln Center Theater Company on Broadway. His two-part stage adaptation of John Irving's *The Cider House Rules* was produced at the Seattle Rep, the Taper, and the Atlantic Theater, and won the American Theatre Critics Association Award. For television, Mr. Parnell was a writer-co-producer for *The West Wing* (two Emmy Award® citations), and writer-producer for a number of others. His award-winning children's book *And Tango Makes Three*, co-authored with Justin Richardson, is published by Simon & Schuster, most recently in a tenth anniversary edition.

DADA WOOF PAPA HOT

a play by Peter Parnell

OVERLOOK DUCKWORTH
New York • London

This edition first published in the United States and the United Kingdom
in 2017 by Overlook Duckworth, Peter Mayer Publishers, Inc.

NEW YORK
141 Wooster Street
New York, NY 10012
www.overlookpress.com
For bulk and special sales, please contact sales@overlookny.com,
or write us at above address.

LONDON
30 Calvin Street
London E1 6NW
info@duckworth-publishers.co.uk
www.ducknet.co.uk
For bulk and special sales, please contact sales@duckworth-publishers.co.uk,
or write us at the above address.

Cataloging-in-Publication Data is available from the Library of Congress
A catalogue record for this book is available from the British Library

Title page logo by SpotCo

Book design and type formatting by Bernard Schleifer

Manufactured in the United States of America
ISBN 978-1-4683-1396-3 (US)
ISBN 978-0-7156-5156-8 (UK)
1 3 5 7 9 10 8 6 4 2

For Justin and Gemma,
the loves of my life

Preface

More than a few years ago, after the production of my play *QED* at Lincoln Center Theater, André Bishop commissioned a new play from me, the subject to be of my own choosing. At about the same time, my husband and I began to talk about starting a family. I had misgivings. When we finally decided seriously, in 2006, to go for it, there began a long process of IVF with our loyal carrier and egg donor. After three attempts, we became pregnant, and in 2009, our daughter Gemma was born.

In the months leading up to that extraordinary moment, my husband and I were often told by other parents, "After you have a child, your lives will never be the same." Although we were prepared for her, like most parents we were also completely unprepared. It only remained for us to find out how.

Dada Woof Papa Hot came about because of feelings and ideas that began bubbling up inside me in the years after becoming a father. The play exists because of Gemma. Its very title, like the main character Alan says, is made up of the first four words Gemma ever spoke.

Although the play's plot of marital infidelity is invented, its psychological themes are autobiographical. As a new parent, I was aware of my basic insecurities about being a father; my worries about who my daughter might be closer to; my competitiveness with my husband for my daughter's affection; my competitiveness with her for his. Having been an only child myself, I was very aware of the potency of a new family member unwittingly creating an "Oedipal" triangle, especially between two parents who had already been together for a long time.

Much to my surprise, I found these insecurities were shared by many parents, both straight and gay, to whom I mentioned them. I also realized that, when we were with other gay dads and moms we only talked about our kids. That was our identity: we were parents first, gay people second. As with many straight parents, our kids were the reason we were becoming friends. This also set me to thinking about what it means to be gay today.

During the time of my writing the play, the gay movement itself underwent a sea change regarding gay marriage and gay parenting. As an older gay man, I came of age first living in the gay ghettos of New York City in the 1970s and 1980s, and journeyed from the celebration of being different and the attempt not to duplicate "heterosexist norms" to something far more integrated. At one point Alan says, "I just don't feel gay anymore." But is this a generational idea? At a later point a different, younger character asks, "Isn't being normal the most radical thing of all?"

The play thus attempts to put some of these questions of gay identity in a new context, but also to find commonality with all parents. All of the characters in the play, both straight and gay, are trying to grab as much love from each other as they possibly can. When she was little, my daughter would often ask each of us, 'Who do you love more? Daddy or me?" In fact, she STILL asks it (she asked it as I was putting her to bed last night). When Alan tells his husband Rob that he sometimes feels jealous of his affection for their daughter, Rob responds, "Do you really think there's only a certain amount of love in the room to go around?" Rob is exposing Alan's childish view of the world. But it's also a very human view, one we all feel at times.

In the play, Alan gives voice to his own sense of incompleteness or inadequacy when he complains that there's more he wants to do in his own life, more he wants to accomplish. He isn't willing to step back and just be a parent as fully as his husband might like. By the play's final scene, Alan's journey from a preoccupation with his own accomplishments to a more selfless way of seeing things isn't complete, nor should it be (that would be unrealistic). But he does learn to worry less about his need to be loved, and more about his daughter's needs. Hers, he realizes, after all, is an ego even more fragile than his own. Were his story to continue, he would hopefully begin to listen to her even more. The love and joy he feels for his daughter might overcome the insecurity he also feels. And, were he to come to feel as confident in his parenting as his daughter wants and needs him to feel, he could progress even farther.

Far enough, perhaps, to someday write a play about it.

PETER PARNELL
June 2016

DADA
WOOF
PAPA
HOT

Dada Woof Papa Hot was originally produced by Lincoln Center Theater (André Bishop, Producing Artistic Director) at the Mitzi E. Newhouse Theater, New York City, and opened on November 9, 2015. It was directed by Scott Ellis; the sets were by John Lee Beatty; the costumes were by Jennifer von Mayrhauser; the lighting was by Peter Kaczorowski; the original music and sound design were by John Gromada; and the stage manager was Cambra Overend. The cast was as follows:

ALAN .... John Benjamin Hickey
ROB .... Patrick Breen
JASON .... Alex Hurt
SCOTT .... Stephen Plunkett
MICHAEL .... John Pankow
SERENA .... Kellie Overby
JULIA .... Tammy Blanchard

ALAN
ROB

JASON
SCOTT

MICHAEL
SERENA

JULIA

PLACE: *In and around New York City.*

SCENE ONE

The bar and front dining area of an upscale restaurant.

ALAN, *50, and* ROB, *mid-40s, are seated at a booth for four.*

ROB

. . . And then he comes in late for the session (again), wearing sweat pants and a tight T that only fits above his midriff, so that his treasure trail is almost completely exposed down to his—

ALAN

Jesus—

ROB

—Yes. And then he says he's hot—

ALAN

(Which he is)—

ROB

(Not like that)—and he sits down, adjusts his, and starts to tell me about how he and his husband did cocaine all weekend, and then they both fucked an old boyfriend of his—

ALAN

My God—

ROB

And he, "S", also actually bottomed—

ALAN

Oh he did?

ROB

By the way, I still can't get used to young gay guys using that word as a verb instead of a noun.

ALAN

Which word?

ROB

Bottomed. "I bottomed for him," instead of "I'm a bottom."

Pause.

ALAN

Could you tell if he was aroused while he was telling you the story?

ROB

No.

ALAN

No you couldn't tell, or no he wasn't?

ROB

No I couldn't tell.

ALAN

Huh. *(Pause.)* And were YOU?

ROB

Aroused? No. No. Yes. A little. What do you think? It was very—

BOTH

Arousing—

Pause.

ALAN

And you still don't think he wants to have sex with you?

ROB

God, no. I think he wants me to admire him like a proud father adoring his gay son. This is all just his way of asking for that. And I keep feeling protective, thinking of him as my baby. Which is probably my OWN defense against wanting to have sex with HIM.

Pause.

ALAN

So you DO want to have sex with him?

ROB

In theory.

ALAN

WHICH theory?

THEY *laugh.*

Are you going to continue to see him?

ROB

I don't know. This was only the third session. Do I even think I have a slot for him?

ALAN (*Slight smile.*)

Oh, I think you've got a slot for him.

Pause.

ROB

Where are they?

ALAN

They're not that late.

ROB

Maybe I should have suggested a closer place.

ALAN

Honey, this place is impossible to get into. They'll be very impressed.

Pause.

I still don't get why we're doing this.

ROB

They're gay. They're dads. One of them's a painter, right?

ALAN

I didn't really get to talk to him.

ROB

Well, now you can.

ALAN

He made me a little nervous, to be honest.

ROB

Look, just promise me you'll keep an open mind about them. And try to be friendly.

ALAN

I'm always friendly.

ROB *gives him a look.*

Well, I'm not *un*friendly. I'm just a little—what do you say? Shy?

ROB

Aloof. At times. *(Pause.)* How did it go tonight?

ALAN

It was—I gave her dinner and played Discovery Garden with her, and then it was time to—and so I filled up the—it only took me like forever to get her into the bathroom, but it seemed to be going okay, and then I started to help her take off her clothes and suddenly, I don't know what happened, she began to scream and I said, "We don't scream in our family, screaming won't get you what you want—"

ROB

Good.

ALAN

—Which only made her scream even more, and then she opened the door and ran out of the bathroom, and the water in the tub was already getting cold—

ROB

Uh-huh—

ALAN

—And I felt like, why is she always like this with me, why doesn't she smile and giggle and stick her fingers in my mouth all-Lolita-like like she does with you—?

ROB

You can't get into a stand-off with a three-year-old.

ALAN

I know that.

ROB

You have to be more inventive—

ALAN

I *know*, it's just that by then I was so totally exhausted—

ROB

(Try this.)

ALAN

(I did.)

ROB

(They're good, right?) Anyway, it sounds like you handled it very well.

ALAN *makes a face.*

It sounds better than last night, anyway.

Pause.

HE *puts his hand on* ALAN*'s.*

I'm sure you were great.

HE *takes out cell.*

I was looking at pictures of her from this weekend. She's so beautiful.

HE *shows* ALAN.

Isn't that great of the two of you?

ROB *turns on movie.*

Sound of little girl laughing.

SCOTT, *mid-30s, buttoned-down, enters.*

ROB *and* ALAN *jump up.*

THEY *all hug.*

SCOTT/ROB/ALAN

Sorry we're/ There you are!/ Hi! Where's Jason?

SCOTT

Coats.

ROB

So great to see you!

SCOTT

So glad we could do this! We *thought* we were going to be on time, but—

ROB

No problem. It gave us time to moon over our daughter.

HE *shows* SCOTT.

We were up at Stone Barns picking pumpkins—

SCOTT

Oh, my God— Adorable—

ROB

And there she is—South Beach. Pool at the Ritz Carlton. We try to go for a long weekend every winter. She loves to swim.

SCOTT

So does Ollie—big fish—

SCOTT *has taken out his own cell.*

Quickly flips through.

Shows them.

ROB/ALAN

Oh, wow.

SCOTT

That's from this summer, in the pool at this house we rented on Fire Island.

JASON *enters. Also mid-30s, but a bit looser.*

JASON

Your wallet.

SCOTT

What?

JASON

You left it in your—

SCOTT

Oh, thanks. *That* would have been a disaster.

ROB

Sit, sit, sit. Split up the couples. Boy girl, boy girl.

JASON

Sorry we're—did Scott tell you? We had a last minute medical thing with baby Clay.

ROB

My God. Is he okay?

SCOTT

Yeah, he has this reflux and sometimes it gets pretty bad, that's all. So we thought the doctor should take a look at him.

ALAN

You took him to the doctor? At seven at night?

SCOTT

No, our doctor makes house calls. Dr. Goldstein. Like, 24/7.

ROB

How amazing.

JASON

Basically, Scott is anxious and calls him at the drop of a hat, and I'm always happy to have him come over, because he's completely adorable.

SCOTT

Jace.

JASON

What? He is.

ROB *(Laughs.)*

A nice Jewish doctor? Who comes to your house? I'd call him all the time, too!

SCOTT *changes the subject.*

SCOTT

This place is incredibly tough to get into. How did you score a reservation?

ROB

So the guy who owns this place has a kid at LVS. He's taught cooking in Nikki's class. She now walks around using the word sautée.

ALAN

He's supposed to be kind of an asshole, but.

ROB

But he and I occasionally bump into each other. So we've become kind of friendly.

SCOTT

We've heard the food is great.

ROB

It is. You should try these, they've got almonds, though—no nut allergies—?

SCOTT

No—

ROB

Good—this guy does amazing things with, this is the best grilled octopus in the city—

SCOTT *(To* JASON.*)*

Hon, wouldn't this be a nice—? We've been looking for a place to celebrate our fifth wedding anniversary.

ROB

Oh, well, if you like it, and want to come back . . . I'm sure we could help you get a rez . . .

Pause.

So. Five years?

SCOTT

Married five, together eight. How long have you guys . . .?

ROB

Married three, together fifteen.

JASON

Fifteen years. Wow.

ROB

We actually dated for almost a year before we got together.

JASON *(Laughs.)*

A whole year?

ALAN *(Slightly embarrassed.)*

I wasn't convinced we were—well, I thought we should just be friends. But Robbie is very smart, much smarter than I am. He knew exactly what was going on.

JASON

What was going on?

ROB

Your basic sex/love split. Endemic to an entire earlier generation of gay men.

Pause.

SCOTT

Anyway, we're so excited to be doing this.

ROB

Yeah. We are, too. The best thing that came out of that gay dads dinner was meeting you guys. We'd never been to any of them.

SCOTT

We'd been to a couple. Jace isn't that into them.

JASON

Face it. Most of the guys look like they've crawled out of a hole somewhere.

SCOTT *shoots him a look.*

(Quickly.) You know, not the most attractive bunch.

ALAN

Why *is* that? Where are all the attractive—?

ROB

Did you talk to those two guys who teach at NYU?

JASON

You mean, those two older guys?

ALAN *(To* ROB.*)*

Older (like us).

ROB

The one in the smoking jacket and the other in the cravat—?

ALAN

Professor Plum and Colonel Mustard. From *Clue*.

ALAN *and* ROB *laugh.*

SCOTT

We used to see them last year on all the pre-school tours. And we'd think, who are these guys? And what kind of strange parents would they—

ROB

And how did we all miss each other back then? Did you apply to LVS?

SCOTT

Yeah, but we never made the lottery.

ALAN

And Oliver is where? Hill & Dale?

JASON

Little Farmhouse. Scott hates it because the first five years, they only give them blocks of wood to play with.

SCOTT

And naked baby dolls.

JASON

Yeah. The kids, like, feed their naked baby dolls blocks of wood. Like something out of Dickens.

THEY *laugh.*

SCOTT

How many pre-schools did you apply to?

ROB

Seven. We went kind of crazy. We'd heard horror stories just about sheer numbers alone.

SCOTT

You ever see that documentary—the one where everybody in New York is trying to get their kid into pre-school—

ALAN

See it? Rob studied it. Rob basically launched a campaign the equivalent to Napoleon invading Russia. Except in this case Napoleon won.

ROB

Alan thinks I'm a little too competitive when it comes to Nicola.

SCOTT

In New York, you can't be too competitive. *(Pause.)* Anyway, it's amazing, right? I mean, three years and never to have run into each other on the street—

ROB

Or in Washington Square Park—

SCOTT

Or at the gym—

ALAN

I think I'd seen one of you, maybe both of you, there at some point . . .

SCOTT

At the gym?—

ALAN

No, the Park. I don't belong to—we have a gym in our building.

ROB

He has a trainer who comes twice a week—Dylan—he's in love with him—

ALAN

Please—he's twenty-five—

JASON

I hate gyms. They're always so crowded.

SCOTT

What do you mean? You like to go to yours when it's the MOST crowded.

JASON *(Laughs.)*

That's not true! *(To* ROB.*)* Although what goes on at my gym, on 14th Street, *is* outrageous.

ROB

Believe me, I hear about it. From my patients. Some of them spend half their lives in that steam room.

Pause.

JASON

Scott mentioned, so you're a shrink? *(*ROB *nods.)* I was in therapy for a while.

SCOTT *shoots* JASON *another look.*

ROB

And did you find it helpful?

JASON

Yeah, *(To* SCOTT.*)* we—did, right?

ROB

Oh. So, you guys were in couples' therapy?

SCOTT

Not now. We were.

JASON *(To* ALAN.*)*
It must be hard not to know who Rob sees. Or about the transferences.

ALAN (*Slight smile.*)
Who says I don't hear a little about them? Marital privilege.

ROB
Identities are never disclosed.

JASON
Are there patients who develop crushes and things on you?

ROB
Yeah. They develop all sorts of things.

JASON *(To* ALAN.*)*
Do you ever see a patient of Rob's whom you actually know—but don't know he's Rob's patient?

ALAN
I could, I guess. But I mean, I wouldn't know, would I?

JASON *laughs.*

SCOTT
If you'll excuse me, I have to—where's the . . .?

ROB *(Points.)*
That way, I think.

SCOTT *exits.*

JASON
Scott gets uncomfortable around the subject of sex.

ROB
Really?

JASON
Have you noticed how gay parents avoid talking to each other about sex? And not just in front of their kids?

ALAN/ROB
Not really./ No I hadn't.

JASON
Anyway, we definitely could have used you over the last six months. If anyone had told us that having a second child was going to be so tough . . . It's just that Oliver was such a good baby. And so when Clay

was so different, we were completely unprepared. Clay was like up all night, screaming his head off. And I developed this, I don't know, anger towards him for suddenly taking over our lives . . .

ROB

Completely understandable.

JASON

And then something happened after about six months, we don't know what. And Clay's turned into this angel. And Ollie's suddenly happy to have a baby brother. So we finally feel like we're back in the world again.

Pause.

Are you guys thinking about having another one?

ROB *and* ALAN *quickly look at each other.*

ROB/ALAN

That is so/ not happening.

JASON

You did IVF, too, right?

ROB *(Nods.)*

We'd thought about adopting. But we decided we wanted to create something of our own, genetically—of our own family—

JASON

We did, too.

ROB

And it had taken years to get Alan to even agree to go through with it in the first place—

ALAN *(Lightly.)*

Not—years—

ROB

So we finally decided—and then—we were so naive—we couldn't match our egg donor with our carrier timing-wise, so we had to freeze the embryos—which didn't take—then we lost our egg donor, and had to—it took three transfers before . . .

JASON

Do you have any more embryos . . .?

ROB

There are six of them still sitting frozen in a petri dish in Morristown, New Jersey.

ALAN

Because Rob refuses to let them go.

ROB

I don't refuse to let them go.

ALAN

We decided we would months ago, and you still haven't—

ROB

It's not that expensive to keep them.

ALAN

Robbie, that isn't the point—

ROB

Look, I know we're not going to have any more. But I guess I'm still holding out some fantasy. Is it too much for me to keep alive a little wish—?

Slightly uncomfortable pause.

Cell rings.

ROB *looks.*

Service. I have to take this. Excuse me.

HE *exits.*

ALAN

He so *would* want another one, if I.

JASON

But you.

ALAN

Like Rob said, it was a big enough deal for us to have Nicola. Not that I'm not thrilled about it, she's incredible, and we're very lucky. I mean, she's got the greatest temperament, and she sleeps through the night, always has, and she loves Robbie to pieces, and he's crazy about her. And me, too. Of course there are things we—I—miss, but there always are, right?

JASON *(Upbeat.)*

Absolutely. It's a whole new world, isn't it?

ALAN

Yeah. On top of which, it's not exactly natural for me, I'm not exactly a natural— I mean, I don't DO things for her. I don't, you know, make her a costume for Halloween, or help her bake Christmas cookies . . .

JASON

Who has the time for that . . .?

ALAN

Actually, Rob does do all that. *(Pause.)* So you're a painter?

JASON *nods.*

What kind of stuff do you . . .?

JASON

Figurative, but subverting figurative, with images of ambivalent blah blah blah.

Pause.

And you, you're a writer?

ALAN *(Nods.)*

Freelance. I've been working on a new book proposal.

JASON

That's fantastic.

ALAN

It's just a proposal. And I've also been writing a series of—

JASON

That's right, you were telling us at the dads dinner, you had just gotten back from, you went to, where? Haiti?

ALAN

Just for a few days. For this article I'm doing about two rival not-for-profit peanut butter companies down there. This American pediatrician started one company to combat hunger out of her rented house in Cap Haitien. Then, after six years, this bigger philanthropic organization contacted her for her recipes and technology, and started producing its own peanut butter. Now the second group has built its own factory, and so they're competing with one another, and there aren't enough peanuts, or frankly enough need, to go around.

SCOTT *returns.*

JASON

Babe, didn't you buy a peanut butter company a few years ago?

SCOTT

You mean, my firm?

JASON

Yeah. Like wasn't there one of those little companies—

SCOTT

That wasn't a little company, Jace. It was Skippy.

THEY *laugh.*

JASON *(To* SCOTT.*)*

Alan was just telling me—he went to Haiti. For some articles he's writing.

SCOTT

Oh, wow.

JASON

What was it like down there?

ALAN

Well, they still haven't recovered. And in Leogane, they're still, I met lots of people who were helping rebuild houses.

SCOTT

And you were away for—

ALAN

Just three days.

SCOTT

And was it the first time you were away from Rob and Nicola?

ALAN

Yeah. It felt strange. I was surprised at how much I missed them. I think I expected to feel more relieved, somehow.

Pause.

Maybe you guys feel that kind of insecurity sometimes. I guess I'm always comparing myself to . . . Like the other day, at the Children's Museum of Art, there was a dad there with his son, adorable kid, about Nikki's age. At one point, Nikki and I went up to the music area, and this boy, Max, and Nikki put the headphones on together and danced around to Coltrane and to the Beastie Boys. Then, the father lay down on the floor and Max took a flying leap into his arms, and they laughed and rolled around on the floor together. I was trying to get Nikki to leave, but instead, she went right up to the dad, and asked if she could jump into his arms, too. He said yes, of course. And she did. And then she kept jumping into his arms, getting up and jumping in again. She did it until finally the dad had to say to her, "Go to *your* dad, *your* dad wants to take you home . . ."

Pause.

And I felt so . . . embarrassed. Like I wasn't the dad she wanted to be with, or something. Crazy, right? Maybe you sometimes feel that way?

Pause.

Or maybe you don't.

ROB *returns.*

ALAN

Everything okay?

ROB

Yeah. Medication patient.

ALAN

Was this "S"?

ROB *shoots him a look.*

I was just asking the letter.

ROB

By the way, our waiter's finally coming back. So—you guys have got to come over to our place soon. And we should plan a play date. In fact, we're taking Nikki to see *Peter and the Wolf* in a couple weeks. Maybe you guys would like to come?

SCOTT/JASON

That sounds fantastic./ That'd be great.

ROB

Nikki's really been getting into being frightened lately.

ALAN

"Early one morning, Peter opened the gate, and went out into the big green meadow . . ."

SCOTT

What?

ALAN

The first line of *Peter and the Wolf.* Isn't that the scariest sentence you've ever heard?

THEY *laugh.*

SCENE TWO

Living room.

MICHAEL *and his wife* SERENA *are having dinner at* ALAN *and* ROB*'s.*

MICHAEL

. . . And, I mean, we would have done anything to like make sure it wasn't him—

SERENA

Michael can't even say the critic's name—

MICHAEL

But with a situation like this you're powerless, you're completely—

ROB

Of course. I have a friend who's a novelist, a very good one, and yet, after a really awful review of a book of his came out, he couldn't get his next book published—

SERENA

God—

ROB

And it's taken him years to—

SERENA

I try to tell Michael, look, your musical made it to Broadway, that in itself is an unbelievable achievement.

ROB

Sure—and I try to console myself with that . . .

ALAN

But that only means it was an even bigger failure, right? A more public failure. Carrying an even greater sense of shame. So how could it help to think that?

SERENA *looks slightly put out.*

MICHAEL *looks uncomfortable.*

ROB *looks at* ALAN.

MICHAEL

Right.

Pause.

SERENA

The risotto was amazing. Your risotto is always amazing.

ROB

Thanks. I made it for Julia Whitty and her husband a couple of weeks ago, and she hadn't told me she was allergic to shellfish.

SERENA

I like the Whittys. They're aptly named.

ROB

I didn't know if they'd take to Little Village School. LVS feels like a more conservative school, like they'd be more of the Hill & Dale type . . .

SERENA

Because she's an actress, you mean?

ROB

Have you seen her new series? HBO? Netflix? It's this comedy, dramedy, whatever—It's good. She plays this mom—you haven't seen it?—whose kids go to this private school uptown—

ALAN

It's all set at Dalton, right?

ROB

Yeah, basically. And she plays this kind of not-so happily—she's got this kind of flaky husband—

ROB

Just like the real thing.

SERENA

What does David Whitty do again?

ROB

Dame Whitty? He's a photographer.

SERENA

Why Dame—?

ROB

Because we're convinced he's gay.

MICHAEL

I know, right?! *(To* SERENA.*)* See? *(To* ROB *and* ALAN.*)* That's just what I've been saying to Serena!

SERENA

You boys are all alike. You think every other man wants to either fight you or fuck you.

SERENA *has been dialing her cell.*

(On cell.) Lucy? Did you give Lizzie a bath? Good. And are you reading to her? Remember, only two books, she'll try to wangle three out of you . . .

ROB

New babysitter?

MICHAEL

Her mom.

ROB *and* ALAN *laugh.*

I'm not kidding. She talks to her like she's the Jamaican caregiver.

SERENA

And don't let Zach stay up after ten—*Babar the King*? Good, but try and skip the racist bits. And what else? *Doctor de Soto*? A masterpiece. I'll text you in a little bit . . . Text, Lucy . . . You don't know what a text is? Ask Lizzie, she'll show you how . . .

MICHAEL

What makes YOU two think David Whitty is gay? I mean, has he ever . . .?

ALAN

Oh, no. He's made far too uncomfortable by us. He tries to seem really relaxed when he's with us. "What's up, guys?" "How's it going, guys?"

ROB

Yeah, it's always "guys".

MICHAEL

I always call you guys "guys", too.

ALAN

That's different. Everybody calls gay guys "guys". He just seems very self-conscious about it.

SERENA

How is that couple you met recently? They have a son who's Nikki's age who goes to Little Farmhouse?

ROB

Jason and Scott. Their son is Oliver. Yeah. They're great. We're just getting to know them. One of them's a painter, the other we suspect is Republican.

SERENA

You *suspect*?

ROB

Well, he's in Private Equity. Fiscally conservative. We like them so much we're afraid to actually ask them about it.

ALAN

We *have* asked them about it. We know how they voted in the last—

MICHAEL

Gay Republicans. With a kid.

ROB

Two kids. But only one of them's a Republican. The dads, I mean.

ALAN

Scott was apparently very helpful in getting the three Republicans to vote for marriage equality in New York State back in 2011.

ROB

Anyway, we really like them. They're a million years younger than we are, like all the parents we meet now. But they're both so sparkly. And one of them's even a little mysterious and sexy.

ALAN

Who?

ROB

Who. Jason.

ALAN

You think Jason's a little mysterious and sexy?

ROB

You do, too. We've talked about this.

NICOLA *(Off.)*

Daddy?

ROB *gets up.*

ALAN

Don't. We agreed.

ROB *sits down.*

NICOLA *(Off.)*

DADDY!

ROB *gets up.*

ALAN

DON'T.

ROB *sits down.*

NICOLA *(Off.)*

DADDY!!! DADDY!!!

ROB *gets up and goes to the hall leading off to* NICOLA*'s room.*

ROB

Nikki, honey, we're just finishing eating.

NICOLA *(Off.)*

What are you eating?

ROB

Grown-up food. Risotto.

NICOLA *(Off.)*

I love risotto.

SERENA

(She knows what *risotto* is?)

ROB

(She's sophisticated.)

ALAN

(She's verbally precocious.)

ROB

(Yes, plus, she *knows* risotto)—Go to sleep, Nicola.

NICOLA *(Off.)*

My twilight turtle went off.

ROB *(To* ALAN.*)*

Her twilight turtle went off.

ALAN

Of course it did. Because it's been 45 fucking minutes.

NICOLA *(Off.)*

DADDY!!

ROB

Would you . . .?

ALAN *gets up, slightly reluctant.*

HE *exits.*

ROB *goes back to sit.*

Pause.

NICOLA *(Off.)*

NOOOO!! I WANT DADDY!!!

ALAN *can be heard trying to reason with her.*

NICOLA *shouts and cries.*

The others eat.

ROB

She's going through a little sleeping thing.

SERENA

They're all like that.

ROB

I think this is related to, we told her you grow when you sleep. And so lately she's been afraid to grow. It'll mean she'll grow old. And she thinks once you grow old, you die. *(Pause.)* Because of Alan's dad.

SERENA

Oh, right.

MICHAEL

Yeah, we were so sorry about—

ROB

Yeah. It wasn't unexpected. And he'd lived a very long life. Anyway, Alan thinks I'm too lenient with her. Well, not lenient so much as merged.

MICHAEL

Merged?

ROB

Yeah. It's a sort of unconscious fantasy of . . .

SERENA

I know what merged means. You needn't worry about it, Michael. You're not merged.

MICHAEL

It's just because Alan's envious Nicola shows you more affection.

SERENA

Honey.

MICHAEL

What? I mean, two's company, right? Somebody's always feeling a little left out? The whole Goldilocks and the Three Bears thing.

ROB

Goldilocks and the—?

MICHAEL

When Serena and I were first talking about having a kid and I was freaking out, we went to this couples therapist and one day I started talking about Goldilocks and the Three Bears. You know, how I was worried about being the odd man out? Being like Goldilocks to the Mama Bear and Papa Bear?

ROB

You mean, being the Baby Bear.

MICHAEL

What?

ROB

Goldilocks is the intruder, not the baby. There's Papa Bear, Mama

Bear, and Baby Bear. Then, Goldilocks comes into the triangle that's already a triangle, don't you see? It's already WORKING as a triangle, it's the FOURSOME that's a problem in that story—

MICHAEL

Whatever. Who cares about the Bear Family? They're bears. Why are we talking about bears?

ROB

You brought it up.

SERENA

Frankly, I think that's one of the reasons we decided to have Lizzie.

MICHAEL

What?! No way. We decided to have another kid because you insisted on having another kid.

SERENA

Yes, because I thought it would be good for Zach. It's harder for only children, I firmly believe that.

MICHAEL

That would be fine, except Zach is almost ten and Lizzie is four. They're not exactly Hansel and Gretel.

ROB

She's been more oppositional lately. It takes forever to get her to do things like get dressed or clean up what she throws on the floor.

SERENA

It only gets worse. The things you end up doing and saying to them. I remember once when Zach was five and having a tantrum. He thought he could outlast me. I looked him square in the eye and said —he was five!—"Zachary, honey. I can break you."

THEY *laugh.*

The screaming and shouting, which has been going on low under, comes back again.

Then it stops.

Pause.

ALAN *re-enters.*

ALAN

She's demanding to see you. She wants you to tell her another scary story.

ROB

God.

ALAN *(Angry.)*

What did you expect me to do?!

ROB

DEAL with her! Figure it out!

SERENA

I'll go with you. I'll tell her a scary story that'll make her head spin like Linda Blair.

ROB *throws down his napkin.*

HE *and* SERENA *exit.*

ALAN*, slightly deflated and exhausted, sits down and smiles quietly at* MICHAEL*.*

THEY *eat.*

MICHAEL

Any news on the book proposal?

ALAN

No. I mean, yes. A couple of rejections. We'll see.

MICHAEL

What's it about again?

ALAN

It's sort of a memoir. About the gay scene, about becoming part of it in New York in the 80s. But I'm finding I can't live there—I can't go BACK there—very easily or happily.

MICHAEL

I loved your peanut butter article in the *Times Magazine.*

ALAN

Oh. Thanks.

MICHAEL

And what's this thing you were telling us at dinner—

ALAN

That I'm working on now? It's an article for *The New Yorker*. About the fidelity gene.

MICHAEL

The fidelity—?

ALAN

Yeah. There are these men who have a gene that's related to the body's regulation of the chemical vasopressin, which is a kind of bonding hormone?

MICHAEL

I didn't know you did science stuff.

ALAN

I do whatever, if asked. Anyway, there are these studies that have shown that those guys who carry the variation in the gene are less likely to be married, and to have serious marital problems if they are. They're now trying to duplicate this research with women.

MICHAEL

Huh. Fascinating.

ALAN

And they're doing these tests. They show people who are faithful pictures of other people, and ask them to rate their attractiveness. Then they're told whether or not those people are interested in THEM.

MICHAEL

I've never been good at renunciation. At abstaining. Who said "the heart wants what it wants"? Tolstoy?

ALAN

Woody Allen.

MICHAEL

Same difference. I've been seeing someone.

ALAN

Then again, the more committed you are, apparently the less attractive you find those who threaten the marriage— Oh. You. What?

MICHAEL

I've been seeing someone.

ALAN
You mean you're—you're having an affair?

MICHAEL
I wouldn't call it that. An affair implies meeting her in a hotel somewhere, long looks, desperate fucks. This is more of a dalliance.

ALAN
A dalliance? Like a chaste kiss in a horse-drawn carriage? Madam Bovary in a fiacre?

MICHAEL
In a what?

ALAN
A fiacre.

MICHAEL
Yeah. Whatever.

ALAN
Still. I'm (shocked). Who is it?

MICHAEL
You really want to know?

ALAN
Of course I want to know!

MICHAEL
Julia Whitty.

ALAN
JULIA WHITTY?!

MICHAEL
Shhhh.

ALAN
Jesus. Julia? What the hell are you—

MICHAEL
What do you expect? Her husband is gay.

ALAN
Aha. So you KNOW that for a—

MICHAEL
No, not definitely, but, I mean—he doesn't pay enough attention to her.

ALAN

Of course he doesn't, according to her. She's an actress.

Pause.

ALAN *is very upset.*

My God. How could you . . .? I thought you were done with all that stuff.

MICHAEL

I AM done with all that stuff.

ALAN

Then what the hell— I mean, your show flops and so you suddenly go in for some immediate idealization?

MICHAEL

I hate that word.

ALAN

Idealization?

MICHAEL

Flops.

ALAN

Are you that insecure that you need someone to romanticize what you do? Granted, the reality of what you do is completely shitty.

Pause.

When do you . . . see her?

MICHAEL

After drop-off. Not every morning. Maybe twice a week.

ALAN

For how long . . .?

MICHAEL

Till pick-up.

ALAN

No. I meant—

MICHAEL

Oh. Since the Fall. Since Julia's series ended shooting. She's had a lot of free time.

ALAN

Hasn't Netflix picked it up yet?

MICHAEL
Yeah. She starts back again in June. Just when Serena and I and the kids go on vacation.

ALAN *(Sarcastic.)*
Oh, perfect. I can't believe you're doing this, and I REALLY can't believe you're telling me about it, and then asking me to collude with you on it!

MICHAEL
I'm not asking you to collude! And why wouldn't I tell you about it? You're my oldest friend since college!

SERENA
Because I'm Serena's friend, too!

MICHAEL
Yeah, of course. Because of me.

ALAN
Why should that matter? I don't want to know anything about you that she doesn't!

MICHAEL
You know A LOT of things about me that Serena doesn't.

ALAN
But how could you put everything—your marriage—in such jeopardy?

MICHAEL
What are you getting so upset about? I mean, I realize you never thought about—you're the only gay man I've ever known who, before you met Rob, lived like a monk.

ALAN
I didn't live like a monk.

MICHAEL
Yes, you did. And now, of course, since all you guys fought for marriage so much, and finally got it, you can't even THINK about not being faithful—

ALAN
I've never said I haven't thought about—

MICHAEL
I mean, it's gay, yeah, but it's still marriage, right?

Pause.

Look, it just happened. I mean, I've been grieving the show. And I have to do it in private. You can't really be sad in front of the kids. They don't get it. Which is good, in that you can't wallow in it. But it does mean you have to hold onto your sadness till the edges of the day. And Serena is sick of hearing about it, which frankly I understand.

Pause.

I look at Serena and think, she's getting older, and I'm getting older. And we're both doing everything possible in our limited power to protect the kids from growing older and getting depressed, while meanwhile we're growing older and getting depressed. And I keep wondering when I'm going to just be with her. All these "false horizons" —when the breast feeding is over, when Lizzie first spends the night in her own bed, when Zach goes to school—but still, there's no release, just farther to travel. But it's Serena, too. I mean, she doesn't WANT to be alone with me. She wants to always be with the kids.

Pause.

ALAN

Are you going to tell her?

MICHAEL

How can I? I mean, I would if I could. I always tell Serena everything. I want to tell her, just so I can ask her whether or not I should tell her.

ALAN

I think you should end it.

MICHAEL

What?

ALAN

End it, Michael.

ROB *and* SERENA *re-enter.*

THEY *look a bit frayed.*

ROB

I just heard a very scary story. Something involving a starfish, a mermaid, and a shark with impulse control issues.

MICHAEL

Serena—

SERENA

What? I got carried away.

ALAN

Is she asleep?

ROB

Fingers crossed. We also read her *The Little Fur Family.*

MICHAEL

What's *The Little Fur Family*?

ALAN

A very strange book that Rob loves. Margaret Wise Brown.

SERENA

I love Margaret Wise Brown.

ALAN

I love SOME of Margaret Wise Brown. Not a big fan of *The Runaway Bunny.*

SERENA

I hate *The Runaway Bunny.* The mother bunny from hell, the "you'll never get away from me" mother. Like *The Giving Tree* and *Love You Forever.*

ALAN

Love You Forever is a deeply sick book. When the mother drives across town with a ladder on her car roof, and climbs up the ladder into her now grown-up son's bedroom window, and rocks him to sleep the way she did when he was a baby . . .?

SERENA

It's always the mother. Talk about parental control and attachment issues. They make Grimm's fairy tales look like Beatrix Potter.

ALAN

Beatrix Potter isn't all that cozy, either. Have you ever READ *The Tale of Mrs. Tittlemouse?*

SERENA *(On cell.)*

Lucy? . . . What do you mean? . . . No, she can't stay up and watch on her iPad, she should be asleep by now . . . And what about Zach? . . . Special rules? What special rules? How can you be so easy on her? Well, you were never that way with me! *(To* MICHAEL*)* She's unbelievable. *(On cell.)* Listen to me. Put him on . . . Hi, Zach, you have to take the lead here, you're Lizzie's big older brother, she listens to you . . . Put Lizzie on. Lizzie? Yes, don't listen to Zach, listen to Nana, sweetie . . . What? . . . Put Nana back on. Lucy? What the hell are you doing? She doesn't get milk after bedtime, she'll pee in the middle of the night . . . And is Zachary now crying? . . . Oh, great. Forget it. We're going. We're coming home, Mom.

MICHAEL *(To* SERENA.*)*

What? Serena, there's nothing wrong—so Lizzie goes to bed late one night, so what?

SERENA

She's completely unable to—it's because of the two of them—my mom can't handle—

MICHAEL

Yes, she can—she raised you and your brother, right?

SERENA

Barely—

MICHAEL

Serena, she's your *mother*—this is your own issue with—

SERENA *(To* THE BOYS.*)*

I'm sorry. We have to go.

ROB/ALAN

Of course./ Are you sure?

MICHAEL

Rob and Alan made this wonderful meal—

SERENA

Which we loved.

MICHAEL

And there's coffee—

ROB/ALAN

It's fine—another time—It's completely/ Don't even think about it . . .

MICHAEL

Well, I'm staying.

SERENA

You should.

SHE *kisses him, starts to go.*

MICHAEL *(Guilty.)*

No, no. I'm going, too.

THEY *say their "thank yous."*

(To ALAN.*)* I'll see you at drop-off.

THEY *leave.*

Pause.

ROB *and* ALAN *stay still for a moment.*

Then, ROB *starts cleaning up.*

ROB

Well, THAT went well.

ALAN

It DID go well. She is so neurotic with those kids.

ROB

BOTH of them are.

ALAN

No, I don't think Michael is.

Pause.

Everything was delicious. The crumble was amazing.

ROB

I'm sorry I was so tense. Having people over always makes me tense.

ALAN

You weren't.

ROB

Yes, I was. Don't—I'll clean that. *(Pause.)* Did you have a good talk with Mike?

ALAN

What? Yeah, fine.

ROB

What did you guys talk about?

ALAN

Nothing in particular. The usual. My career, his career.

ROB

I hope he gets out of his funk soon. He should really be on something. It's been driving Serena crazy.

ALAN

Everything in her life is wrapped up in those kids. I think that marriage is in serious trouble.

ROB

I'll do that.

ALAN

Where does the wine thing go?

ROB

You mean the corkscrew? In the top left drawer. I never know whether it's you or Sophia who misplaces all my kitchen supplies.

ALAN

It's me. I never know where things go.

Pause.

Was Serena freaked out about how difficult Nikki was being all night?

ROB

Nikki wasn't being difficult.

ALAN

Yes, she was. Before bed she wouldn't look at me when I asked her to clean up, and she kept sticking her tongue out at me—

ROB

Which I've told her not to do—

ALAN

And then she hit me. It was when I tried to put her pajamas on, and she started to scream, so I said to her—

ROB *(Weary.)*

Look, I really don't think I can listen to—

ALAN

—And so I pulled her pajama top on and she was fighting me and so her hair got caught—

ROB

Poor kid.

ALAN

Poor kid?! Why poor kid?! I'M the one who got hit in the face. *(Pause.)* I wish you wouldn't always take her side.

ROB

I don't.

ALAN

You do it a lot.

ROB

Because she's powerless.

ALAN

Powerless? She's the most powerful person in the room.

Pause.

ROB

Your agent will find you a publisher, Alan.

ALAN

What? Oh, Yeah. *(Pause.)* What made you think of that?

Pause.

I was looking at the Scottish landscapes before. The ones we bought when we were driving through the Isle of Skye. They made me weep.

ROB

They're so beautiful. It was so beautiful.

ALAN

Those trips we used to take. Cornwall.

ROB

The Tresanton Hotel.

ALAN

Venice. The Christmas before Nikki was born.

ROB

You were an absolute wreck. AND you froze your ass off.

THEY *kiss.*

ALAN

We should try and get away somewhere together. Just the two of us. We haven't since Nikki. Almost four years.

ROB

Yeah. That would be . . . But who would stay with her?

ALAN

Sophia.

ROB

She sees Sophia all week long. If only we had a family . . .

ALAN

We don't. We're old. Everyone we're related to is either demented or dead.

Pause.

ROB

We'll figure it out. I'm going to bed.

HE *picks up a design magazine.*

New *Elle Décor*. Porn.

ALAN

I'll finish cleaning up.

ROB

You going to stay up and work?

ALAN

No. I have Dylan in the morning.

ROB

He gonna work that body?

HE *grabs* ALAN.

THEY *hug. Kiss.*

ALAN

You haven't talked about "S" for a bit.

ALAN

Not having enough sex at the gym?

ROB

I'm actually a bit worried about him.

ALAN

Has he taken his T-shirt off in a session yet?

ROB

I'm serious.

Pause.

ROB *looks at* ALAN, *smiles.*

Kisses him.

ALAN

HAS he taken his T-shirt off in a session?

ROB *grabs* ALAN.

ROB

Could you . . . that's not appropriate, okay?

THEY *grapple. Hug.*

ROB *gently dislodges himself.*

Do we have plans for the weekend? Did you contact Scott and Jason? About going to the zoo, or—

ALAN

I haven't heard back from them.

ROB

Do you want to text them?

ALAN

Now?

ROB

Whenever. *(Pause.)* I want us to get close to them. We like them.

ALAN

Yeah. We do.

Pause.

ROB

Are you coming to bed? *(Pause.)* Come to bed.

HE *kisses* ALAN.

Quickly. Before the Ambien starts to kick in.

HE *exits.*

ALAN *alone, watches him go.*

HE *takes out his cell.*

HE *writes a text.*

HE *sends it.*

SCENE THREE

NIKKI'*s room.*

A mix of adult and children's things. Stokke crib, stuffed toys, a rocking horse, a Radio Flyer wagon. Books.

ALAN *is showing* JASON *the room.*

JASON

Oh, yeah, it's great.

ALAN

But you see, we still haven't fully—this used to be my study—

JASON

Uh-huh—

ALAN

Where I did my—some of the books are still—

JASON

Yeah, I see. *The End of Wall Street* next to *The Very Hungry Caterpillar.*

ALAN

That was for an article I was doing on the history of Goldman Sachs.

JASON

Really? Which book?

Pause.

You got the Radio Flyer.

ALAN

Yeah. Nikki liked playing with it so much at Ollie's house.

JASON

Ollie likes riding on it with Nikki.

Pause.

Everything looks so—Swedish.

ALAN

Rob likes everything to be simple and elegant. Fisher-Price shall never darken our door.

JASON

Well, good luck with that. We thought that, too, but when Ollie was six months old he got sent a Fisher Price piano and he wouldn't let it out of his sight. There's a reason all these kids' toys are purple and pink and look like they've been farted out of Dr. Seuss' ass.

Pause.

Do you mind if I—?

JASON *sits on the floor.*

ALAN

We could go out to the—

JASON

No, no. This is fine.

ALAN *(Laughs.)*

Really?

ALAN *sits, too.*

JASON

I've gotten sort of used to everything happening at this height. Besides, it feels good to sit. Great that we ran into each other after drop-off. I usually don't pass LVS on my way home from Little Farmhouse. You and I will have to do this more often, now that we know . . .

JASON

I only drop her off two mornings a week. Robbie does one, and Sophia two—

JASON

Sophia is great.

ALAN

So is Thu. She's from—

BOTH

Tibet.

JASON

Easy to control. That's why Scott likes her.

ALAN

Rob would, too, for that reason.

JASON

It's terrific that our caregivers get along so well. Nice especially when they're from two different—

ALAN

Cultures, yeah—

JASON

You wait and see, we're going to make Nikki and Ollie boyfriend and girlfriend yet. Start them early. Fifteen years from now they're going to look back and realize this was where their love came from.

ALAN *(Laughs.)*

Actually, if we put them together too much, we'll probably pretty much guarantee they're NOT going to become boyfriend and girlfriend. The incest taboo. If anything, they'll start to think of themselves as brother and sister.

JASON

Forget it, then we should keep them as far apart as possible!

Pause.

ALAN

Nikki didn't seem a little down to you? At drop off?

JASON

Down? No, not at all.

JASON *looks at photographs.*

She always looks so happy.

ALAN

She's with Robbie there. They're so crazy about each other. Like two people completely in love.

JASON *(Points.)*

That's—?

ALAN

That's Robbie at the age Nikki is now. With his mom. They were devoted to each other.

JASON

And *that's*—

ALAN

That's Nikki.

JASON

Amazing.

ALAN

Right? The physical resemblance—

JASON

So then, Rob is the biological . . .? I mean, Scott and I, we just assumed . . .

ALAN *(Nods.)*

We both created embryos, but it's pretty clear whose took. *(Pause.)* Actually, that's not true. It's what we tell people—what we agreed to tell people. But. We didn't use embryos containing my . . . We only used Rob's. He'd done all this research and found out there was a greater risk of autism with slightly advanced paternal age.

JASON

And that didn't bother you?

ALAN

Not really, no.

Pause.

Anyway, she seemed a little down to me. But it could have just been her cold—

JASON

Nicola has a cold?

ALAN

Well, getting over one.

JASON

Oliver had one last week—

ALAN

I think maybe Nikki got it from Oliver?

JASON *(Nods.)*

I had it first, then Ollie, now Scott's got it, too.

ALAN

I get sick all the time now.

JASON

So do I.

THEY *laugh.*

ALAN

I was sorry not to see Scott. This morning.

JASON

He's in DC. Been traveling so much lately, for work.

ALAN

I have to admit, I don't quite get what it is he does.

JASON

Neither do I, frankly.

THEY *laugh.*

And you said Rob . . .?

ALAN

Usually Thursdays. But this morning he had a very early patient.

JASON

Somebody's got to work!

ALAN

I work.

JASON

Oh. Yeah. I wasn't implying—

ALAN

—And it isn't always easy with the type of stuff I've been doing lately—

JASON

Of course—that you write at *all* is—

ALAN

Well, that you paint at all is—

JASON

I know—

ALAN

But it's been especially difficult now that—

JASON *leans over and kisses* ALAN.

Longish kiss.

THEY *part.*

ALAN *looks down.*

JASON

Sorry. Was that . . .? Did I misunderstand? I've had an inkling, the past few weeks. And then, when you invited me over here for coffee . . .

ALAN

Yeah?

JASON

To see if I wanted to see Nikki's *room* . . .?

ALAN

Well, not just her room. Our place. Hadn't you been asking . . .?

JASON

No.

ALAN

Oh. I thought—

JASON *kisses* ALAN *again.*

JASON

Was that still . . .?

ALAN

It just feels weird. Under the circumstances.

JASON

And what circumstances are those?

ALAN

That we're married, not to each other but to other people, that we have kids the same age, that our kids are becoming friends, and that we're parents, playing the role of parents—

JASON

Playing the *role* of parents—?

ALAN

Not the role, I don't mean the role, we're *actually* parents, I just meant that's how we know each other, in our *capacity* as parental . . .

Pause.

Anyway. It feels strange.

JASON

I think it's kind of hot, actually. Like we're doing something really furtive. Secret.

ALAN

I just don't want you to think it's because I'm desperate or anything. I mean, I'm not some bored housewife who's moping around her life. I'm not Kate Winslet.

JASON

Really? Because I suddenly feel like Patrick Wilson. Want to go down to the laundry room and fuck on the washing machine?

Pause.

Actually, we wouldn't. Fuck, I mean. It's not part of the rules.

ALAN

The rules?

JASON

We have rules, Scott and me. Well, I do. I mean, we both do, technically, but Scott would never act upon them. We set them up after we first got together, and kept them . . . at first, it bothered Scott, so we went into therapy together. Eventually, we sort of worked out an understanding. Then we both decided we wanted to get married . . . So they mostly come down to what I can and cannot do. And fucking is definitely a cannot. Whereas kissing, squeezing tits, getting blown—but not blowing—fingering—but not licking—ass are allowed.

ALAN

That last one must have taken a lot of negotiating.

JASON

You have no idea. Anyway, basically everything else isn't.

ALAN

Whatever else that leaves.

JASON

Quite a lot, actually.

ALAN

And what about enjoying—or not enjoying—it? Getting close—or not getting close—falling—or not falling—in love? Where do they place?

JASON

Yes to enjoying, no to everything else, obviously. I'm happy to limit it to the gym. Because I just like—I just need—sex.

ALAN

And how did you get Scott to agree . . .

JASON

It was the only way he could get me to go along with having a baby.

Pause.

ALAN

You mean, you didn't want . . .?

JASON

Yes, sure, but not in the same way he did.

ALAN

Yet you agreed to have a second one.

JASON
Yeah. Because, guess what, I found out I like being a father.

ALAN
And you find having affairs don't interfere—

JASON
They're not affairs. They're just sex. Casual sex. Safe casual sex. And not ALL that often. And never on the weekends.

ALAN
And have you done this with other gay dads before?

JASON *(Laughs.)*
No. You're the first. *(Pause.)* Does that completely freak you out?

ALAN
No. Not. Completely.

Pause.

Maybe it's a mid-life thing. A mid-life *suburban* thing. Although we're not in Maplewood, New Jersey.

JASON
But we could be. Give us a couple years.

ALAN
Funny. It's like we're suddenly both involved in two traditional marriages. Mine is the usual one—husband who feels wife is more involved with the child than with him, jealous of the child for taking wife away; yours is the husband who has affairs on the side—if affairs can include getting blow jobs in steam rooms—and wife politely looking the other way. Actually, yours is really the husband who's openly gay by virtue of the fact that he's married to a man, publicly imitating straight behavior while privately practicing Old School gay behavior. An out gay person's story that's just like a not-out gay person's story. And that's what we now call liberation . . .

Pause.

When I was first coming out, in the early 80s, and everyone was having sex with everyone else, and we were all part of the gay ghetto, I was the guy who wanted to be faithful and monogamous. To my boyfriend who'd go out and get drunk and dance and come home the next morning and tell me, the guy I met last night said he was a writer, too. I saw the movie *Making Love* and thought, what would be so bad about being Michael Ontkean and meeting Harry Hamlin and setting up house with him instead of Kate Jackson? That was what I aspired to.

JASON

And look at you. That's what you got.

ALAN

Yeah. And I'm very, very lucky. I got through the epidemic. Only one small thing happened. I never ever imagined I'd get married and become a parent.

Pause.

I just don't feel gay anymore. Not in the way I used to feel.

JASON

Because of not having extramarital sex that you never had, anyway?

ALAN

I guess. Because becoming like everybody else isn't EXACTLY what I wanted, either.

Pause.

Nikki's first words were dada and woof and papa and hot. Not as a sentence, as separate words. Dada for Rob, woof for dog, papa for me, hot for the radiator. But Rob and I joked, if you put them together—Dada Woof Papa Hot—they say what every gay dad wants to hear.

Pause.

A couple of weeks ago, we were actually fucking—a rare occurrence these days—and Rob was about to come, and Nikki woke up from her nap. "Daddy!" she called—And he was past the point of—so he quickly came and then pulled up his pants and went running out to see her. Afterwards, he couldn't remember whether he'd come or not. It was as if the two most powerful parts of his brain—sex and parenting—were both being turned on at the same time. I kept on jerking it, but . . . I sort of lost my erection after that. I had to think about somebody else— *(Pause.)* I thought about you . . .

Pause.

JASON *looks at him.*

I remembered where I'd seen you, before we met. I had seen you a couple of times with Oliver in Washington Square. I thought you were a DILF.

JASON

(?)

ALAN

A Dad I'd Like To—And then, one time, I was with Nikki, and I walked by you, and I let myself—I looked at you for the briefest—I cruised you. And I thought you cruised me back.

JASON

I might have. I don't remember. But. Yeah. I might have. I probably did.

JASON *leans in again, kisses him. It becomes more passionate.*

ALAN

Not here.

JASON *gently pushes* ALAN *down his chest.*

ALAN *stops.*

Not. Here.

JASON *pulls* ALAN *up.*

Sees that ALAN *is weeping.*

JASON

Do you want me to go?

ALAN

Yes. No. I don't know.

JASON

I'll take that as a maybe, and let myself out.

HE *starts to exit.*

Oh, yeah. We're on for ice-skating on Saturday.

HE *exits.*

ALAN, *alone.*

ALAN

Wait. WAIT!

Pause. JASON *returns.*

HE *stands, far apart.*

THEY *stare at each other.*

SCENE FOUR

Outside music classroom.

Violin playing one note, off.

ROB *is outside, looking in.*

ALAN *enters.*

ALAN

Hey.

ROB

You came.

ALAN

My meeting finished early. What are you doing out here?

ROB

Rehearsal. Parents not allowed. Min Sun sent me out. Nikki was having trouble concentrating.

ALAN *(Looks.)*

She's not actually going to play, is she?

ROB

No. She's not going to play. She's just going to stand there and hold the violin under her chin.

ALAN

And you think it's a good idea?

ROB

The concert? Yeah. Why?

ALAN

Because she's just going to be—standing up there. In front of an entire audience.

ROB

That's the Suzuki Method. She'll start to get a sense of discipline, of what it feels like to perform.

ALAN

That's just it. It's so performative. She's just turned four. And we're not Asian. *(Pause.)* You know what I mean. I feel like we're shoving it down her throat.

ROB

Look, I've always said, if she doesn't like it, she doesn't have to do it. But she's going to do great, you'll see.

Piano heard, off, playing "Twinkle Twinkle Little Star".

ALAN

Jesus. Look at her, just standing there.

ROB

Adorable. She sees you. She knows we're watching. Smile.

ALAN

I am smiling.

ROB

Wave.

THEY *wave at her.*

ROB

Do you have your I-phone?

ALAN *takes it out.*

HE *makes a movie.*

HE *turns it on* ROB.

Say something, proud Daddy.

ROB

She's our little Jascha Heifetz.

ALAN

Only an ancient person would know who that is.

Piano and violin, off.

ROB

Look. She's playing just for fun. See?

ALAN

God, what a screech.

THEY *laugh.*

ROB *watches.*

ALAN *touches him.*

ALAN

I'm sorry I've been so prickly lately.

ROB

It's okay.

ALAN

No, it's. I don't know what comes over me some times.

Playing, off.

ALAN

You do love me, don't you?

ROB

Of course I love you, noodle.

ALAN *kisses him.*

Not here.

ALAN

Why not?

ROB

We're at Third Street Music School.

ALAN

So?

THEY *kiss.*

(Pause.) Promise me you won't leave me. Ever.

ROB *(Laughs.)*

Leave you? Where would I go . . .? *(Pause.)* She's finished. Here she comes! *(Calls.)* Hi, sweetie!

ROB *exits.*

ALAN *waits a moment, follows after.*

SCENE FIVE

Playground.

ALAN, MICHAEL, *and* JULIA WHITTY *are sitting and standing, watching their kids, off.*

THEY *drink coffee,* ALAN *and* MICHAEL *eat muffins.*

ALAN *seems vaguely uncomfortable.*

JULIA

. . . So they're both married, and they're both having this affair, right, but it's like everything else, they've backed themselves into a corner, they're just locked into another kind of marriage—they can't get out of it—

MICHAEL

Your character is very, the whole show is very well written.

JULIA

Sure, Eric's a genius. That's why I agreed to do it, even though I never thought, I mean, even though it's Netflix and supposed to be classy, who really gives a shit about parents? I mean, there's no violence—

MICHAEL

Except emotional—

JULIA

Right—and the sex scenes are kind of steamy. Although just once I'd like to do an extra-marital sex scene in which we both get into bed and fall asleep because we were up with our kids all night and we're just too exhausted. *(Shouts.)* Jared! SHARE!

Pause.

And you said you haven't seen it?

ALAN

Not yet, no.

JULIA

There are gay characters—the young ones are trying to figure out commitment while still having lots of uncommitted sex, and the older gay married couples are completely idealized—

ALAN

I didn't realize there was gay sex in it. Now I'll definitely have to see it. Rob and I tend to binge watch.

JULIA

Like everybody these days.

ALAN

We're still getting through the first season of *The Wire*. Anyway, it's on our queue. Instant. Prime. Whatever.

JULIA

JARED! Give him the truck!

MICHAEL

Alan? You okay?

ALAN

Yeah. Sure. Why? Because I thought you and I were meeting up for a play date with the kids, and I didn't expect . . .?

MICHAEL

What?

JULIA *(Laughs.)*

Me. I don't think Alan likes me very much.

ALAN

What? That's not true. I like you fine, Julia.

JULIA

Do you?

SHE *smiles.*

MICHAEL *looks at* ALAN, *not sure how to take this.*

Anyway. Sorry if I'm a bit strung out, you guys. It was one of those, get the shoes on the boys and get them out the door mornings, and David was NOT being helpful—

MICHAEL

Any reason?

JULIA

He's got this photo shoot for some German magazine for like their Fall issue, Lord only knows why they have to do it so far in advance, and so he was up at six taking pictures of strangulated Thanksgiving turkeys . . .

MICHAEL

Strangulated?

JULIA

Plucked, skinned, heads and beaks twisted—

MICHAEL

Jesus—in your kitchen?

JULIA

Scared the hell out of the boys. Except for Jared, he loved it. And then Harry and Caleb came roaring downstairs at like seven . . .

ALAN

You have three? I didn't realize—

JULIA

Yeah, well, one from my previous— And David from his— And David promised to take two of them to soccer practice and the third to baseball this afternoon—

MICHAEL

David's so athletic, whenever I see him at school he's like, heading off to basketball or rock climbing or cycling—

JULIA

He loves sports—

ALAN

(Reaction formation.)

MICHAEL

(What?)

ALAN

(Nothing.)

JULIA

I can barely ever get him out of his running shorts.

ALAN

I can believe that.

Pause.

JULIA *lowers her head for a moment.*

JULIA

Look at how nicely Nikki and Lizzie are playing together.

MICHAEL

Girls.

ALAN

Well, friends.

JULIA

Nikki is so great.

ALAN

She is, she's yeah.

JULIA

She's got such spunk.

ALAN

Spunk. That's the word.

JULIA

It must be nice to have a girl. I sometimes think I'll go crazy with the three boys. It's a zoo all the time.

MICHAEL

Girls can be worse.

JULIA

After the age of ten. But I'm glad for David's sake that we have boys. Do you think you'd have felt more comfortable having a boy? Or maybe you plan on having more than one, so—

ALAN

No, we don't. Plan on having more than. And no, I don't think I'd feel more comfortable with a boy.

MICHAEL

All the baseball and soccer, right?

JULIA

Well, that's not exactly, though yeah—

JULIA

That makes sense.

ALAN

What makes sense?

JULIA

That you'd be more comfortable being with a girl.

ALAN

I didn't say that.

JULIA

Oh, I thought you just said—

ALAN

No. I said I didn't think I'd feel more comfortable being with a boy. I didn't say I'd feel more comfortable being with a girl. I think I'd feel just as uncomfortable being with a boy as I do being with a girl.

THEY *laugh.*

MICHAEL

Fathers and sons are definitely different. Lizzie is head over heels about me, and me her. But Zach is actually, well, I think Zach is actually my best friend.

ALAN

Really.

MICHAEL

Besides you. I mean, I like to THINK of him as a best friend.

ALAN

You like to think of your ten-year-old as your best friend?

MICHAEL

Sure. When it comes to taking walks and playing soccer and shooting hoops and shit.

ALAN

That's because you're still a ten-year-old boy yourself. Who just happens to write show tunes. *(To* JULIA.*)* But Julia, WHY do you think it would make sense that I'd be more comfortable being with a girl?

JULIA *(Laughs.)*

Oh. I don't know. Just because . . . dressing her up, and.

ALAN

Ah. Yeah. Actually, that's more Rob's thing. I should be better at, I don't even dress myself. I wear all of Rob's clothes.

JULIA

Really? Because everything looks so good on you. And you have such good taste, too.

ALAN

Rob.

JULIA

David has great taste in clothes. He loves to go shopping. He's worse than I am, actually. All my clothes get picked out for me for the show. And I just take everything home. If it were up to me, I'd just wear sweat pants all day long.

MICHAEL

You look good in sweat pants. You, well, you look good in everything.

JULIA *laughs a bit nervously.*

JULIA

Really? Thanks.

MICHAEL

Maybe you just need to be looked at differently.

JULIA

By who?

MICHAEL

By somebody other than David.

Pause.

JULIA

Oh, God. There's Rina Baldwin. From the second year Green Room class. Jared got into a fight with her son Marshall last week and wacked him in the face with a dump truck. *(Smiles, calls.)* Hi, Rina! *(Beat.)* If looks could kill. She's seen Jared, she's taking Marshall right out of there.

MICHAEL

You want to go apologize?

JULIA

I already have. Three times. AND sent Marshall like a year's supply of gummy bears. There's just so much more I can do.

Pause.

If she ever found out, she could do some real damage.

ALAN

Found out what?

JULIA

Nothing. *(Pause.)* I hate the way everybody knows everything about everybody in our school.

MICHAEL
What do you mean? Nobody knows anything.

ALAN
I agree. For instance, Michael doesn't like to think about the fact that gay men are always throwing themselves at him. I'm sure a few dads, even at school, wouldn't mind. A few closet cases.

MICHAEL *shoots him a look.*

JULIA *laughs.*

Aren't I right, Julia?

JULIA *(Laughs.)*
I have no idea. I don't even THINK there are any closet cases.

ALAN
You don't?

JULIA
Who? Wally Crawford? Larry Stackhouse? *(Laughs.)* I mean, I consider myself a pretty good detector of—and, in my line of work, I certainly know a lot of— Then again, the world is changing so fast. I mean, look at you guys. That you and Rob are married, that alone is incredible. When I was in school, the idea that two men . . .

ALAN *(Simply.)*
Yeah. That's true . . .

JULIA
And I'm sure I'm not THAT much younger than you— And then that you could have a BABY? And I thought it was women who were supposed to have it all! Turns out it's you guys. Well, we'll see what comes from that.

ALAN
What do you mean?

JULIA
No, just that—the old adage, be careful what you wish for. I mean, pretty soon, when gay marriages start to break up . . .

MICHAEL
That's an optimistic, hopeful thought, Julia—

JULIA
Maybe not, but I'm just being realistic—human nature—

ALAN

Julia's right about that. In fact, I've been thinking of interviewing some couples for an article I'd like to write about gay divorce.

JULIA

One day soon young gay men and women are going to wake up and figure out why being married and having kids is so tough. For one thing, they're going to figure out you have to be rich, especially if you're living in New York, and you have to have enough living space, which is even tougher. And being married will still mean dividing time between work and being a parent, and between loving one person and loving a number of people, and between being independent and being tied down. I mean, I'm sure you and Rob are blissfully happy—although like you say, nobody really knows anything about what goes on between two people—

ALAN

I never said that—

JULIA

But if you want gay marriage, and gay children—

ALAN

Did I say I wanted gay children?

JULIA

No, sorry, I didn't mean gay children,—I meant, children of gay people—well, you're welcome to all that goes along with it—

ALAN

Like what?

JULIA *(Shouts.)*

JARED! STOP HITTING HIM! *(To* MICHAEL*)* Like everything! Like every. Little. Thing.

Pause.

ALAN

It's just, when it comes to gay men, now that everybody can have THIS life, why would anybody want THAT one?

JULIA

Which one?

ALAN

The life of running around. Of hiding.

JULIA

I agree.

ALAN

Of course, everybody still hides.

JULIA

Everybody? Like who?

ALAN

Like everybody

JULIA

I don't hide.

ALAN

You don't? But you're an actress. You're a professional hider. Professionally, and otherwise. Right?

JULIA *looks at him.*

JULIA

You know? *(To* MICHAEL*)* He knows? You told him?

MICHAEL

Kind of.

JULIA

Jesus.

ALAN

Yeah. That's how I felt, hearing about it.

JULIA

Why did you—?

MICHAEL

He's my best friend.

JULIA

So what?

ALAN

That's what I said. Believe me, if I had known, I wouldn't have wanted to know. But he can't help it. He's an asshole, Julia.

MICHAEL

No, I'm not.

ALAN

No, he's not. He's just a little oblivious.

JULIA

Well, THIS is a little awkward.

ALAN

Not really. It shouldn't be. Angering, yes, for you and for me. For you because I know, and for me because Serena is one of my best friends, too.

MICHAEL

You're critical as hell of Serena.

ALAN

That doesn't mean anything. I'm critical as hell of everybody.

Pause.

Look, I'm sure you have your reasons for having an affair with Michael. And I can only guess at what some of those might be.

JULIA

I'm sure you think David is gay, don't you?

ALAN

No, I don't.

MICHAEL

Yes, you do.

ALAN

So do you.

MICHAEL

No, I don't. I never said—

JULIA

And what if he were? Do we have to pigeonhole everyone? David and I have a good marriage. Do I know everything about him? No. Does he know everything about me? Clearly not. I'm not deluding myself. And I'm not living a lie. Whereas you . . . from what Michael tells me . . .

Pause.

ALAN

What has Michael told you? *(To* MICHAEL*)* What have you told her?

MICHAEL

Nothing—

JULIA

That's not true—The thing about David is, David is incredibly sweet and kind and a fantastic father, and as a matter of fact, a very sexual person—very generous in bed—very loving and generous and also actually quite uninhibited, some of the things he likes to—

MICHAEL

Julia, Jesus—then what the fuck are we doing here?

JULIA

What do you mean? We're watching our kids.

MICHAEL

No, I mean, you and I—

JULIA

What do you think we're doing? We're helping each other.

ALAN

Now Rina Baldwin really IS looking . . .

Pause.

She has such a disappointing child.

Pause.

Have you ever thought about why so many people have a second child when their first is about three? Sure, it's because the first kid is out of the woods. But I think it's also because when you see what your first kid is turning out to be, you think, maybe I should try and roll the dice again. You'd never admit it to yourself, but you think maybe, just maybe . . . I can do better. Maybe I can get the child I actually fantasized I'd get.

JULIA

That's a terrible thing to say.

ALAN *laughs.*

My first marriage was pretty much a disaster, but I put a lot of hope and faith in all my children. Goodbye Michael. Nice to see you, Alan. Come on, Jared, we're leaving.

SHE *exits.*

MICHAEL

Julia! Wait!

Pause.

Thank you very much, asshole.

ALAN

Me?! What about you?! I can't believe you told her—something I told you in strictest confidence—

MICHAEL

Yeah, well—

ALAN

It was one moment—*once*—and it was over before it—

MICHAEL

Why did you say those things to her?

ALAN

What things? Look, she is seriously sick. She is using you to end her marriage.

MICHAEL

You've got to be kidding me. She just told us she's very happy with him.

ALAN

That's so not true. She's so defended. She's clearly miserable with him.

MICHAEL

YOU'RE the one who's projecting. What are you so angry about?

ALAN

I'm not angry.

MICHAEL

You've been angry for as long as I've known you. You just cover it over with a lot of nice. *(Calls.)* Lizzie, honey! Time for a snack! (*To* ALAN*)* And I'm not paying for the donut.

HE *exits.* ALAN *watches him go.*

SCENE SIX

Beach house.

Late afternoon.

Childrens' voices, far off.

ROB *and* SCOTT *come in from outside.*

SCOTT

. . . He loves the water, I just think he's going through this weird thing right now where he's afraid, maybe because he fell when that wave came in, and so he's scared about getting knocked off his feet . . .

ROB

Completely understandable.

SCOTT

I mean, what else would you suggest we do . . .?

ROB

I'd throw him in, probably. Head first.

SCOTT

No, you wouldn't—

ROB *(Laughs.)*

Joking, Scott, just—

SCOTT *(Laughs.)*

Oh, right—

ROB

We're lucky that Nikki's pretty fearless. But she fell ice skating last winter, and it took her a couple of times of our trying to get her back on the ice before she'd do it again.

ROB *looks out.*

ROB

Gosh, they're like little specks out there. I feel so guilty being away from them.

SCOTT

What do you mean? Erica's with them.

ROB

That Erica is a godsend.

SCOTT

She's great, right? She's saved our ass so many times this summer—I'd love to take her back to the city with us—

ROB

But what about Thu?

SCOTT

Thu is wonderful, but all that Tibetan calm is beginning to get on my nerves.

ROB

Where does Erica go to school?

SCOTT

BU.

ROB

Too bad.

SCOTT

Yeah. Next summer, if there is a next summer, we'll try and get her to do it again. It really makes a difference.

ROB

What do you mean, if there is a next summer?

SCOTT

Nothing. Just. If we decide to summer out here again, as opposed to going someplace else.

ROB

Where would you go?

SCOTT

I don't know. We haven't really had a chance to talk about it yet.

ROB

Because maybe it would be something we all would—

SCOTT

Yeah. Oh, yeah. That'd be great.

Pause.

Who stayed with Nikki when you two went down to South Beach last month?

ROB

She went to our friends Michael and Serena's, we've told you about them, they have an older boy and a girl almost Nikki's age—?

SCOTT

Of course.

ROB *(Laughs.)*

I'm afraid that was so not a vacation, from Alan's point of view—I was on the phone every other minute with Nikki, and then apparently Michael fed her so many sweets she ended up spending the first night throwing up. He took them all to a matinee of *Matilda* and they ate candy the entire two and a half hours. We've found out that kids' matinees of Broadway musicals are basically junk food conventions.

SCOTT

Speaking of.

SCOTT *hands* ROB *chips.*

ROB

I couldn't, I'm already breaking all the rules.

SCOTT

You're being so good. No desserts. No dairy.

ROB

I've become really boring.

SCOTT

Not at all. I envy your willpower. But does that mean you won't have a beer?

ROB

A little too early for me. Oh, what the hell.

SCOTT *hands him a beer.*

Pause.

SCOTT

Michael and Serena. They're the ones having marital trouble?

ROB

Well, they're, yeah, at the moment, they're.

Pause.

SCOTT *looks away.*

Scott? Is everything okay?

SCOTT

What? Oh. Yeah. Sure.

ALAN *comes in.*

ROB *looks out.*

ALAN

They're running in and out of the waves now.

SCOTT

Look, Clay's going to stay asleep at least for another half hour or so. Why don't you two go?

ROB

No, no, you haven't had any time away from—why don't YOU go and we'll—

SCOTT

You guys didn't come out here to babysit, and besides, Ollie loves being with Erica, he's got a huge crush on her, which frankly cheers me up because it means he won't be gay—

ROB

Hard to tell at age four—

SCOTT

I know, and then Jace will be back soon . . .

Pause.

ALAN

Where did Jace go, anyway? He disappeared like right after lunch.

SCOTT

He went to see a friend.

ROB

Somebody here? In the Pines? You mean, like, a collector?

SCOTT

Not, not a collector. Though he's got a couple of those, too, out here.

ROB

Things have really taken off for him, right?

SCOTT

Yeah. That little group show in Chelsea in April really. Yeah. He has a terrific dealer now. The art world is so completely fucked up.

Pause.

ALAN *looks out.*

ALAN

Jesus. There's a guy next door who has the most amazing—he must be like twenty-three.

ROB *looks.*

ROB

He looks like your trainer.

ALAN

You think?

ROB

Dylan has a prettier face. And is also probably a better person.

SCOTT

Your body has definitely gotten more solid looking, Alan.

ALAN

I'm training with him like three times a week. My shoulders hurt, my legs are killing me. Never looked better; never felt worse.

ROB

It's the only way he can have a relationship with Dylan. It's all sublimation.

ALAN

This guy has definitely shaved his ass.

JASON

Welcome to the Pines.

ALAN

I never really liked the Pines. The first, and I believe the last, time I came out here was with my first boyfriend, who insisted on having sex in the bushes and who wanted to go home with everybody, and did. This would have been in 1983. Sort of parade's end.

SCOTT

Jason would have loved to have been gay in those years.

ROB

Who wouldn't?

ALAN

I wouldn't. I didn't. And I was. It was actually kind of awful. Everybody debauching with everybody else. Except me.

JASON *enters.*

JASON

Hey, guys.

SCOTT

You're all wet.

JASON

I took a quick dip in the ocean before coming back up. Out to that little spit beyond the cove.

JASON *wipes himself dry with his towel.*

SCOTT

You get a little dirty?

JASON

There was some kind of oil beyond the breaker, some kind of dark shit, maybe I'll quickly—

SCOTT

Use the one outside, the baby's still sleeping.

JASON *takes off his clothes.*

ALAN

You visit the kids on the way up?

JASON

The kids told me to get lost. They're having their last swim of the day with Erica.

ROB

We've been replaced by the mother figure.

SCOTT

Can you blame them?

ALAN

You know, I always worry that Nikki doesn't get to see enough vaginas. She sees Sophia's, and Rob's sister's, when she visits from Portland. But that's about it.

SCOTT *passes* JASON.

JASON *kisses him.*

JASON

Hey.

SCOTT *(Cool.)*

Hey. I think I'm going to start cooking.

JASON

I'll fire up the grill.

SCOTT

No, I'll do it.

ALAN
That salmon was amazing last night.

SCOTT
So you won't mind more fish? After Rob's incredible lobster salad for lunch?

ALAN
Hey, we're at the ocean, right?

ROB
Nikki won't eat fish again, but maybe we can throw some hot dogs and hamburgers in for her and Ollie?

SCOTT
Sounds good.

JASON
So did Scott tell you? If this deal comes through that he's been working on for months, it'll be a big thing for us.

SCOTT
Jace—

JASON
What? It will. It's practically done. If it happens, next summer we'll have our own house—

Music heard, off.

SCOTT
Here they go again. Jason?

ROB
I can't believe, after the run-in you had with them yesterday—

SCOTT
Why did they take a house on the quiet side? Isn't it enough we have to make up all kinds of stories for the kids about why they see guys lurking in the bushes?

ROB *(Laughs.)*
I loved that you told them it's a lot of dads being friendly with one another.

SCOTT
Dads with no kids. They weren't buying it.

ALAN
Hasn't Ollie ever walked in on you guys in the middle of sharing some tender moments?

SCOTT

Not yet.

ROB

Nikki did once. We told her Papa was looking for his socks at the foot of the bed.

Baby heard crying, off.

SCOTT

Shit.

JASON

I'll go talk to them. After my shower.

HE *exits.*

SCOTT

Can you guys excuse me a sec . . .?

HE *exits in the opposite direction.*

ALAN

Is something going on between the two of them?

ROB

I have no idea.

ROB *goes to* ALAN.

HE *hugs him.*

SCOTT

You okay?

ALAN

Yeah. She's just being so impossible with me this weekend.

ROB

I know. I'm sorry.

ALAN

It's like I'm afraid to even touch or hold her, for fear she's going to start shouting "No!" at me again. God, she can be so exhausting!

SCOTT *re-enters.*

SCOTT

He's okay. I told him, there, there, the noisy homosexuals will quiet down soon. This is why I didn't want to take the house here again this summer. Well, one reason.

Music gets lower.

There we go.

CLAY *quiets down.*

SCOTT *goes back to preparing.*

ALAN

Funny. When you handed Clay to me yesterday . . . it felt so odd. I mean, I forgot how to hold him. Amazing what you forget as your kid grows up.

SCOTT

You forget *everything.*

ALAN

I can't even remember Nikki ever being that tiny.

JASON *re-enters.*

JASON

Their group has, like, expanded exponentially. A whole bunch more young ones have arrived. All in various states of undress.

SCOTT

And I'm sure you'd like to join them?

JASON *shoots* SCOTT *a look.*

ROB

Can you believe in a month we're all going to be applying to kindergarten?

SCOTT

I know. I wish we could keep Ollie at Farmhouse for another year. Applying to kindergarten just feels too much right now, what with work, and . . .

JASON

Yeah. Besides, Ollie's definitely grown very attached to his wood blocks. What about you guys?

ROB

I'm dreading the competition. It's going to be even tougher than pre-School.

JASON

You still thinking in our neighborhood?

ROB

Yeah, but I'm also thinking our chances are better as a gay couple uptown. Double diversity points—we're two dads AND we live downtown!

ALAN

I don't like the idea of Nikki commuting so far. I'll have to schlep her up there at like 7 am. Which would cut into my writing time. Not to mention feel pretty disruptive to her.

ROB

There's a school bus. And all the parents say the kids love the school bus.

ALAN

But that wouldn't be until she's older. Besides, they grow up fast on the school bus.

ROB

I grew up fast in Rockland County.

ALAN

Yeah. Right.

ROB

Look, I just want her to go to the best school possible.

JASON

But how do you know what's best, when they're too young to know what they're like?

ALAN

Exactly. Unless it has something to do with status.

ROB *(Tight.)*

It has nothing to do with status. It does have something to do with money.

ALAN

They're ALL expensive. So why, since we live in a good catchment, wouldn't she go to PS 41?

Pause.

ALAN *and* ROB *slightly tense.*

JASON

How was Washington? Alan said you guys were going down to see your egg donor?

ROB

Yeah. It was wonderful. We'd prepared Nikki, told her who she was, of course. And she understood, but only, you know . . . to a point. But we think it was a good thing to do, right, sweetie?

ALAN

Yeah.

ALAN *looks away.*

Pause.

Strange, to suddenly be alone without the kids.

JASON

That's why I like it out here. Ollie can stay at the beach all day. I get a lot of work done. I've stayed out here with them during the week even, while poor Scott has had to labor in the fields.

SCOTT

It's nice for me, too, sometimes. Having the apartment in New York all to myself.

Pause.

ROB *looks at* ALAN *for a moment.*

ROB

Can you even remember what it was like, being a couple before we had kids?

SCOTT

I can't.

ALAN

I can. It was wonderful. Sleeping late, going wherever you want, reading books, seeing plays, having sex—

ROB

Yeah, but you get tired of all that.

THEY *laugh.*

ALAN

And not competing all the time for your husband's attention. Or being dumped on by your daughter.

ROB

Poor Alan gets the worst of it.

SCOTT

Still?

ROB

And you boys don't have this? Ollie doesn't favor one of you over the other?

JASON

No. Must be a girl thing. Oliver likes to share us.

SCOTT

If anything, I'm the one who doesn't like to share. At least, I don't like to share Jason. And I have to share him all the time.

JASON

With who?

SCOTT

With everybody. With you tell me.

Pause.

Anyway, it doesn't matter. The important thing is the kids. What's good for Ollie and Clay, you know. I mean, you hear people say this all the time, but once you have children, all your other problems seem so small, suddenly everything else pales in comparison. Its their vulnerabilities, their pain, their loss that you . . . In fact, I almost feel like when I see them suffer the tiniest disappointments, the struggles that mean getting through an ordinary day, whether it's putting on a shoe or deciding which side of the street to scoot down . . . it makes me fall in love with them all over again, maybe when I love them the most . . . because they are trying so hard to claim some kind of power . . . Some small sense of who they really are . . .

Pause.

HE *looks down.*

ROB

Scott? Are you okay?

SCOTT

Fine, yeah. I'm. No, not really.

Pause.

HE *turns to* JASON.

It's just. I can't do this anymore. I just can't.

JASON

Honey—

SCOTT

Do you want to tell them where you were all afternoon? Or should I?

JASON

No, I don't. Why should we?

SCOTT

Because they're our best friends.

JASON *(Suddenly hard.)*

It's none of their business.

Everything stops.

Pause.

SCOTT

He was with his boyfriend. Jace has a boyfriend.

ALAN

What . . .?

SCOTT

And I've been trying to live with it, I mean, what couple doesn't go through this sometimes, right? I just never expected it would be something that got more serious— I suppose I knew at some point this was going to . . . I mean, if you play with fire. Of course there might be someone he'd fall in love with—

ROB

What do you mean, at some point?

SCOTT

I mean this time. As opposed to all the other times.

ROB

There were other times?

JASON

So now you know, you can all crucify me.

SCOTT

I don't want to crucify you. I just don't think I can take it anymore. I am quite sick of it all. Really. Sick of hearing about you and him and his boy.

ROB

He has a boy toy?

JASON

No, a *boy*—his son—he's married, too. To another guy. With a cravat.

ALAN *(Realizes)*

Oh.

ROB *(Quietly.)*

The gay dad's group?

ALAN

Professor Plum? Oh, my God—

SCOTT *(Laughs.)*

Crazy. Right? This summer has just been—and the thing is, he hasn't been neglectful of the kids, if anything, he's been even more attentive. Which is why, in a way, I've tried to endure it. I mean, all my life, it's been, maybe it's because I grew up in such a conservative, and maybe you're right, maybe I am just duplicating heterosexist normative behavior in having wanted marriage and family and the whole thing, but I don't care! And anyway, isn't being normal the most radical thing of all?

Pause.

I'm sorry. I'm just.

Pause.

You know Jason was the first guy I ever . . .? The ONLY guy I ever . . . I mean, I didn't even know I was gay until I met him! It's my fault. For not being a liberated enough gay man.

JASON

Okay, so what can I! I've told you! It happened! And the last thing I ever thought was that somebody I didn't even find particularly attractive . . . Not at first . . . And somebody who's also a dad?

SCOTT

I don't want to hear it. It's so clear you have a problem. And you're just too weak or too lazy to figure it out—After all that we've built together!

JASON

What we've built together is here. It's still here!

SCOTT

No, it isn't. Because it needs both of us to hold it in our hands. And you're NOT here.

JASON

Scott, please—

SCOTT

And I can't take how selfish, how completely selfish—

JASON

Don't.

SCOTT

You never think things out!

JASON

BECAUSE I CAN'T. I CAN'T. ALWAYS. THINK. THINGS. OUT. I don't always know what door is going to open, and when. I know that's being irresponsible. But sometimes we do things—even those of us who DO think things out— DO THINGS—

SCOTT

Well, you did. And now it's over! You hear me!? Over!

HE *exits into bedroom, slamming the door behind him.*

Music goes up again, off.

JASON *goes to the door.*

JASON

Scott! Scott! For Chrissakes!

HE *bangs on the door.*

Scott! Open up!

ALAN

I'm sorry.

Pause.

JASON *looks at* ALAN.

JASON

For what? This has nothing to do with you.

ROB *(In a neutral tone.)*

He's very emotional right now but maybe later I'm sure you two can find some way to talk this through . . .

JASON

Please cut the shrinky bullshit tone, Rob, okay? You don't know as much as you think you do . . .

ROB

Now hold on.

Pause.

ALAN

Another married guy?

JASON

What can I say? You opened the door.

ROB

What are you talking about?!

JASON

I'm the one who's sorry. It's me. I'm fucked up.

ROB

What are you talking about?!

Pause.

Oh, God.

ALAN

Nothing happened, Robbie.

JASON

Nothing??

ALAN

NOTHING HAPPENED!!

Sound of children's voices.

ROB

Keep them out.

JASON

What?

ROB

KEEP THE CHILDREN OUT!

JASON *(Calls.)*

Come on, kids! We're going out to grill!

HE *exits.*

ALAN *and* ROB *stare at each other.*

ROB

Shit.

SCENE SEVEN

ALAN *and* ROB*'s bedroom.*

Night.

ROB *is sitting up in bed, watching television.*

Cell rings.

HE *clicks off.*

Sighs.

HE *gets up and exits.*

Front door, off.

ROB *re-enters, followed by* ALAN.

ALAN

Sorry. I knew you'd be— I've been gently knocking. I didn't want to wake Nikki.

ROB

I didn't realize the door was locked from the inside.

ALAN

Nikki must have—

ROB

Yeah. She had a lot of trouble going to bed tonight. Kept thinking there was a wolf just outside the apartment.

ROB *gets back into bed.*

She was asking again where you were.

ALAN

What did you tell her?

ROB

Papa's away for a few days, researching a story. She wanted to know where, she wanted to know when you'd be back. She wanted to believe . . . whatever I could make up.

Pause.

ALAN

Season Three?

ROB

Yeah. Omar is a great character. He's going after Stringer Bell.

ALAN

You started without me.

Pause.

I needed some books. I'll just get them.

ROB

You need them tonight?

ALAN

I'm on a deadline.

ROB

For what?

Pause.

ALAN

How is she?

ROB

She's great. I took her to Lily's birthday party on Saturday and she wore her jeans with her tutu over them, and she and I danced what was the most amazing sort of pas de deux and hip hop and afterwards she told me when she grew up she wanted to marry me—

ALAN

Can we talk?

ROB

We are talking.

ALAN

No, I mean.

ROB *turns off the TV.*

HE *looks at* ALAN.

ROB

How's the hotel?

ALAN

It's fine, it's. You know. Michael is finishing work on a new show, and so he's up all night, with the headphones on. Kinda hard for me to sleep in the other room.

ROB

It's oddly fitting that you two bozos ended up with each other. If I were Serena I'd kick his ass out completely, for good.

ALAN

But our situations are completely different—

ROB

Who cares about the details? Or do you think what you did wasn't a betrayal?

ALAN

Of course it was, but I've tried to explain . . . I don't expect you to understand why it happened.

ROB

I don't want to talk about this again—

ALAN

And I felt so badly after—you have no idea how badly—

ROB

It's all so fucking middle class—

ALAN

Well, we're fucking middle class!

ROB

Just do me a favor and tell me why—

ALAN

Because I wanted something that was mine. All mine.

ROB

All yours? Are you kidding me? Another married man? With a sex addiction? How was THAT all yours?! Whereas everything that is here —everything you see in front of you—EVERYTHING HERE IS YOURS!

Pause.

Who are you? Just some asshole who got selfish?!

ALAN

Does getting selfish automatically make you an asshole?

ROB

Usually, if you're not the child anymore!

ALAN

Look, I know it's childish, but things have changed. And sometimes I feel you don't love me as much as you love her.

ROB

Jesus. Do you think there's only a certain amount of love in the room to go around?!

Sound of NIKKI, *off.*

NIKKI *(Drowsy.)*

Daddy . . .? Papa? Is that you?

THEY *freeze.*

ALAN *(Whispers.)*

She's still asleep.

ROB *(Whispers.)*

Yeah.

THEY *continue to whisper.*

Your narcissism is unbelievable.

ALAN

You always said I was an inhibited narcissist.

ROB

Yeah well, how's that rage working out for you?

ALAN

I can't help it. I see you look at her the way you used to look at me. And then she rejects me as the one she doesn't want to be with—Do you know what it's like to constantly hear "Go away, Papa! I hate you, Papa!"

ROB

She also tells you she loves you! She doesn't want to be with you less. She thinks she wants to be with me more. We've talked and talked about this, it's the Oedipal struggle—

ALAN
I don't care what you call it! It's fucking hard to live with!

ROB
Nobody's denying that. But that's true of everyone, and it's going to change. It's a natural part of her development.

ALAN
But what if it doesn't? Maybe it's not the same as with a man and a woman, maybe with two guys the child latches on to one parent and rejects the other—

ROB
"Rejects"! She doesn't reject you!

ALAN
Of course she does, Rob—

ROB
She's a 4 year old!

ALAN
She's almost 5!

THEY *involuntarily laugh.*

Then, serious again:

ROB
This is YOUR issue! It's not hers!

ALAN
Look, you're competitive, too.

ROB
So I'm competitive! We're two different people!

ALAN
Yeah. And we're also both men!

ROB
What the hell difference does that make?

ALAN
Who knows? Nobody's done the research yet!

ROB

Look, *you're* the one who feels ambivalent—you're the one who feels separate from us.

ALAN

Oh, it's us now!

ROB

Yes! Why do you feel separate from her AND from me? Why?!

ALAN *(Blurting it out.)*

I don't know why! Maybe because she ISN'T mine! Not completely!

ROB

What?!

ALAN

I mean, because I'm biologically not—

ROB

Oh, for God's sake—

ALAN

—Because YOU'RE the one who's her flesh and blood!

Pause.

ROB

Oh. Is that what this is . . .?

ALAN

I know that's a terrible thing to say. I didn't think it would matter. I mean, I didn't even want to be a father to begin with. So how could it matter?

ROB

Jesus, Alan—we talked about this—you know why we did it—

ALAN

Yes—

ROB

And you agreed—I asked you—I BEGGED you to search deep in yourself—

ALAN

And I did! But would it have made a difference? You wanted a child, and you wanted YOUR child!

ROB

That is so unfair—

ALAN

And now I feel left out. Because she doesn't feel like mine!

ROB

But she *is* yours! She DOES love you! Why can't you just accept that?

ALAN

I want to. I do. But sometimes I can't help feeling that she's driving us apart. And we can't only be about her. We can't.

Pause.

ROB

You have never forgiven me for wanting to have a baby.

ALAN

Maybe I haven't. I don't know. I miss us.

ROB

So do I.

ALAN

I miss being enough for you. *(Pause.)* Why wasn't I enough for you?

ROB

You WERE enough for me.

ALAN

No. I wasn't. *Why* wasn't I?

Pause.

ROB

It was as if I looked at our life, moving forward, and I felt as if nothing was going to change. We'd continue to spend our days together doing all the things we love to do. And we'd grow old together, looking at each other . . . That would have been the old story. The old gay story. The happy, then a little sad gay story. And it would have been wonderful. But also lonely . . . Can two people love each other and still feel lonely together?

Pause.

And there was always this thing in me . . . When I was about eight or nine, my mother asked me what I wanted to be when I grew up, and

I told her, a father. Although what I actually thought was a "mother." But I couldn't say that, of course. And now, when I look at Nikki . . . I see my mother . . . She's in there, somewhere . . .

ALAN

Yeah . . .

ROB

In her face, but also the way she moves her arms and hands, the way she laughs and tilts her head . . . and in the shape of her body . . .

ALAN

Yeah. I see it too, all the time . . .

Pause.

It hits ROB.

ROB

Oh God, I miss my mom. I miss her so much. We had such a thing.

HE *lowers his head.*

Now Nicola is all I have of her.

ALAN

And deep inside I guess I think, Nikki must know . . . And one day, she WILL know . . .

ROB

And do you think it will make a difference to her?

ALAN

I think it will. I suppose I think it will actually, finally, make sense to her.

Pause.

ROB

Nikki looks at me the way my mother used to look at me whenever she'd see me. A great smile would spread across her face. Nobody else has ever looked at me like that.

ALAN

I look at you like that.

ROB *looks at him.*

ROB

No. You don't.

Pause.

ALAN

I haven't yet achieved what I've wanted to in my life.

ROB

And saying THAT—after I said what I just said—is exactly why you don't look at me the way I want you to look at me.

Pause.

ALAN

Robbie, what are we going to do?

Pause.

Remember last fall, after we took Nikki to see *Peter and the Wolf*? She was so scared . . . it was like the stupidest thing for us to do. She loved it, but she was scared. And how could she not be? She was afraid of the wolf. Who isn't?

Pause.

ROB

You have to be strong for her. You *have* to be. We have to be.

ALAN

We have to be.

ROB

Otherwise, it just won't work.

SCENE EIGHT

Restaurant.

SERENA *sits alone.*

ROB *enters.*

SERENA

I was early.

ROB

No, you weren't. You were on time.

THEY *kiss.*

SERENA

Alan with you?

ROB

Coats.

SERENA

Michael's still at rehearsal. He's running late. Nicola okay?

ROB

Yeah. She was exhausted. These longer days, with swimming and play-dates . . .

SERENA

I know. It gets to a point where you're happy to see them practically falling on their feet.

Pause.

SHE *turns away.*

ROB

I can't believe how long it's been. You look good.

SERENA

Thanks. So do you.

ROB

Is everything . . .?

SERENA

Yeah. We're good. We're . . . it's been a little strange. But he's, we're, you know, hanging in. And that bitch actress. She seems to have adjusted to her new . . .

ROB

Yeah.

SERENA

Too bad about David Whitty.

ROB

I wouldn't feel too sorry for him. The guy he's dating lives in baronial splendor facing the toy boat pond on 5th Avenue.

SERENA

I know. Michael says he's living in the Frick Museum.

THEY *laugh.*

Pause.

I don't know which makes me angrier, that Michael had an affair, or that he had it with an actress. So lame. Now that it's over—that I insisted he end it—after I found out about it . . .

Pause.

I feel like the amount of work it takes to keep Michael afloat, to make sure he doesn't sink under the weight of his own insecurities . . . Now that he's back in rehearsal, I'm in for it again. I always forget what hell it is.

ALAN *enters.*

THEY *kiss.*

Amazed you guys got a reservation tonight.

ROB

We love it here.

ALAN

We haven't been here in a long time. Not since . . .

HE *stops.*

Oh. Right.

HE *looks at* ROB.

We, uh, took those two friends, that couple, here. Jesus. Almost a year ago.

SERENA

I was sorry to hear about them. Do you know if they're still—?

ROB

Together? We don't think so.

SERENA

It's so sad.

ROB

Yeah.

SERENA

And those kids!

Pause.

Maybe they'll work things out.

ROB

Yeah. Maybe.

MICHAEL *enters.*

THEY *all hug.*

ALAN

How was rehearsal?

MICHAEL

Good. You know, awful, but.

SERENA

That's why you're work-shopping it.

MICHAEL

Yeah. It feels good to be back in rehearsal again. This is the hopeful time. Before everything turns to shit. I have no idea what's going to happen. I feel like I have no control—over anything anymore.

ROB*'s cell.*

ROB

It's Sophia . . . Hi Sophia, is everything okay? . . . She wants to say goodnight . . . Hi, sweetie . . . Yeah, we're at the restaurant . . .

ALAN

Say goodnight for me . . .

ROB *nods.*

ROB *(Exiting.)*
Yeah, we'll be home after we have dinner with Aunt Serena and Uncle Mike . . .

ROB *exits.*

SERENA *watches* ROB *go, takes out her cell.*

SERENA
You guys don't mind, I'm going to call . . .

MICHAEL
Don't hassle your mother, Serena.

SERENA
I won't. I'll—just check in.

As SHE *exits:*

(On cell.) Hi Lucy . . . Yes, they can both watch for TWENTY minutes, but NO Nickelodeon. It makes them obnoxious.

MICHAEL
How are you?

ALAN
Fine. You?

MICHAEL
Good. Better, now.

ALAN
I'm glad that—

MICHAEL
Don't say anything. It was—stupid, I know. The whole thing was stupid.

Pause.

I'm glad you and Rob . . . I'm glad you guys are. You know. Okay. *(Pause.)* You ARE okay, aren't you?

ALAN
Yeah. I think—I hope—we will be . . .

Pause.

I've gone back to working on my book.

MICHAEL

Really?

ALAN

Yeah. I decided to just write it without worrying about whether it'll get published, or if anyone will ever read it.

MICHAEL

Is it still about the '80s?

ALAN

Yeah, but it's not JUST about the '80s anymore. It's actually more about Nicola and me, really. About my feelings about being a father.

MICHAEL *(Surprised.)*

Being a father? You?

ALAN *(Laughs.)*

Yeah, I know, right?

Pause.

MICHAEL

How IS Nicola?

ALAN

She's great.

MICHAEL

I mean, how are you and Nicola?

ALAN

We're good. We're. It's a, you know.

Pause.

It's funny. After I came back—I found out how much Nicola missed me —how she was so happy to see me . . . which was nice, because who doesn't want to feel wanted? And then, last week, I dropped her off at school, and waved at her through the classroom window. I went like this *(Indicates* I "HEART" YOU*)*—and she mouthed something back that I couldn't understand. She said it again, and still I couldn't—And then she pressed her face against the glass and said it a third time and I finally heard her ask: "Will you always love me?" And I was so shocked. "Will I always . . .? Yes, yes, of course, sweetie, always, forever and ever!"

Pause.

I think I've been worrying about whether she loves me enough, when all along . . . it's HER need to be loved that I should be worrying about.

Pause.

I could have lost . . . everything. It's so fragile, what we have, so easy for it all to disappear, if we just happen to wander the wrong way out into the . . .

HE *lowers his head.*

God, Michael, I'm so scared. Of all of it. Of something happening to her, of Rob and me growing older, of one of us going before the other. But for as long as we have each other . . . for as long as I have them both. . . I need to hold them so close . . .

Pause.

ALAN *looks out.*

That girl over there. With her parents. How old is she, do you think?

MICHAEL

Eight? Ten?

ALAN

Yeah. Eight. Ten.

MICHAEL

What is it? Alan?

HE *stares at her.*

ALAN

Nothing. Imagining. Just, imagining.

Pause.

ROB *comes back in, holding phone.*

ROB

She wants to talk to you.

ALAN

What?

ROB

She wants Papa to say goodnight to her.

ALAN *takes the cell.*

ALAN

Hi, sweetie . . . Night night . . . I love you . . . Can I what? . . . Can I tell you a scary story? Now? Of course I can tell you a scary story. Of course I can . . . But not TOO scary . . .

Pause.

Which one? Yeah. "Early one morning, Peter opened the gate, and went out into the big green meadow . . ."

END